MESSENGER CAT CAFÉ

MESSENGER CAT CAFÉ

NAGI SHIMENO

Translated by M. Jean

HARVILL

1 3 5 7 9 10 8 6 4 2

Harvill, an imprint of Vintage, is part of the Penguin Random House group of companies

Vintage, Penguin Random House UK,
One Embassy Gardens, 8 Viaduct Gardens, London SW11 7BW

penguin.co.uk/vintage
global.penguinrandomhouse.com

First published in Great Britain by Harvill in 2026
First published in the United States of America by Putnam,
an imprint of Penguin Random House LLC, in 2026

Copyright © Nagi Shimeno 2022
English translation copyright © M. Jean 2026

The moral right of the author has been asserted

Originally published in Japanese as *Dengon Neko Ga Cafe Ni Imasu /
伝言猫がカフェにいます* by PHP Institute, Inc. in 2022

English edition arranged with PHP Institute, Inc., through
Emily Books Agency LTD and Casanovas & Lynch Literary Agency

Book design by Nancy Resnick
Title page illustration by Andrew Rybalko/Shutterstock

No part of this book may be used or reproduced in any manner for the purpose
of training artificial intelligence technologies or systems. In accordance
with Article 4(3) of the DSM Directive 2019/790, Penguin Random House expressly
reserves this work from the text and data mining exception.

Printed and bound in Great Britain by Clays Ltd, Elcograf S.p.A.

The authorised representative in the EEA is Penguin Random House Ireland,
Morrison Chambers, 32 Nassau Street, Dublin D02 YH68

A CIP catalogue record for this book is available from the British Library

ISBN 9781787305441

Penguin Random House is committed to a sustainable future
for our business, our readers and our planet. This book is made
from Forest Stewardship Council® certified paper.

CONTENTS

Prologue · *1*

TASK ONE
Messenger Cat Goes to a Gallery
3

TASK TWO
Messenger Cat Sees a Chocolate Cake
63

TASK THREE
Messenger Cat Plays in a Field
107

TASK FOUR
Messenger Cat Basks in a Playground Breeze
149

TASK FIVE
Messenger Cat Curls Up on Someone's Lap
191

Epilogue · *235*

MESSENGER CAT
CAFÉ

PROLOGUE

They say that when animals or people pass away, they become stars. If you look up at the sky, you'll always see them.

The truth is, they aren't really that far away.

Life and the afterlife are connected. The slightest of openings exists between them. So it's actually pretty simple to come and go between the worlds.

That said, if just anyone went waltzing back into the land of the living, it'd cause some shock, for sure. It must be done carefully. The trick is to slip through, nice and smooth—and remain undetected.

You could say I'm a work in progress in that regard.

TASK ONE

MESSENGER CAT GOES TO A GALLERY

1

I woke up to the sound of the lecture hall's closing bell.

"Whew," I said with a sigh. "Finally, it's over."

I extended my front paws and arched my white-striped, caramel-colored back as far as my chair allowed. When I glanced to my side, I noticed Natsuki, a black cat, making an annoyingly studious expression and muttering to herself.

"Tenet one: Sleep early, wake up early. Tenet two: Get proper exercise. Tenet three: Do not overeat. Tenet four: Take care of your own needs. Tenet five . . ."

Just a few moments ago, our brown tabby lecturer had recited those rules—the Five Tenets—for living in this world.

"You take this stuff too seriously," I told Natsuki, finishing my stretch. "Those are the same rules we lived by before. There's no reason to call them the 'Five Tenets.'"

Natsuki glanced up at me. Her eyes were practically spinning. I thought they might pop out of her head.

"But Yuna took care of me until now," she complained. "I don't know how I'm ever supposed to take care of my own needs . . ."

Yuna was Natsuki's human. Former human, I supposed. She'd adopted Natsuki from an acquaintance's house when Natsuki had been only two months old. At the time, Yuna lived alone—she had just graduated college and gotten her first real job. Years later, when Natsuki was twelve, Yuna got engaged, and both of them moved in with her fiancé. Thankfully he'd loved cats, too. He and Yuna took care of her together for about five years, until Natsuki eventually came into this world at eighteen years old.

"Just don't start sobbing," I said, trying to give off an air of seniority, but I wasn't managing my emotions well, either.

Was Michiru okay? Was she attending her college classes? She'd always talked about how uncomfortable she felt going to school. Was she getting along with her friends?

Ever since she was little, Michiru had been shy, not to mention quick to cry. Her teary-eyed face surfaced in my memory and made my heart clench.

I hopped down from my chair with an extra spring in my step to hide my sniffle.

2

I'd arrived in this world in the morning, three days ago.

I couldn't remember my cat parents. I faintly recalled shivering on a cold patch of concrete (which I'd later learned was a bicycle parking lot for an apartment building). It had been a frigid night. All I could do was curl up into a ball. Papa had been on his way home from the office when he'd found me. If he hadn't taken me in, I would've been sent here a lot sooner.

After that night, I lived with him and Mama—and Michiru, who was a baby at the time. I spent nineteen years as their pet cat, which was a long life in that world, and I was proud to say that I'd died a natural death in my golden years.

I got to know the black cat Natsuki this afternoon. She must've just arrived, because I'd caught her wandering around, unsure of what to do. So I talked to her.

I assumed she'd been spoiled growing up. She was sent here with so many toys, she needed two arms (legs, in our case) just to haul them around. A brightly colored stuffed bird—her favorite, apparently—had hung from her mouth. Though she hadn't looked like the toy comforted her all that much. I'd felt sorry seeing her like that, so I figured I'd help her out.

To officially join this world, one had to first attend a training seminar, or "guidance" of sorts. I'd been scheduled to attend the one this afternoon, so I brought her along with me.

Now that the training seminar was over, Natsuki had a lot to say.

"Don't you think it's cruel that we can't go see our humans for the next seven months? I wanna see Yuna right now," Natsuki complained, still gloomy.

"You'd only scare her if you went too soon. You have to wait," I reasoned.

"The lecturer said the earth would 'warp,' right?"

"That was a weird way to phrase it. I think he meant this world and that world would become unbalanced if we alerted anyone to our presence. Deceased humans can go back during the Obon festival, and even get close enough to observe while the living practice the seven days of Higan. But us cats get some flexibility, too, once our first seven months are up."

"When exactly is seven months from now again? Let's see . . ."

Natsuki counted on her toes, though they didn't have the right joints for counting, so she extended her claws to get the job done.

"January," I deadpanned. "I'd counted several times since I'd come to this world. I knew it by heart at this point.

"Oh, thank goodness. I'll make it in time." She dropped her long, tense tail with a flop of relief.

"Make it in time for what?"

"Yuna's baby. It's in her tummy right now. I wanted to be there when she gave birth."

I nodded with approval. "Good for you."

Her tail wiggled like jelly as she collected her excessive array of toys.

"Let's go look at the bulletin board in the hallway," I suggested, already making my way over.

"Good idea. We need to look for work."

"Yeah. We've got to pay our own way for food and housing and all."

Room and board wasn't a *real* worry in this world. We could find stability fairly easily. But if we wanted to eat the tastiest treats or play with the best toys out here, we needed to make our own living.

"You're lucky you're a black cat," I told Natsuki, glancing at the board. "Black cats are in high demand. Look."

I leaped up on my hind legs so that my front paws landed on one particular flyer: a HELP WANTED notice.

"Wow, you're right. A lot of these jobs are limited to black cats," she replied, squeezing her bird plushie. Black cats were popular choices for café mascots, picture book characters, movie appearances, and other various visually related jobs.

"Not to mention you'll get busier once summer is over," I added.

Natsuki looked confused. "Why's that?"

"You'll be helping with Halloween."

"Like those cats that ride on broomsticks?" Her ears pricked. "I'd love to be like them!"

I tore my gaze away from Natsuki's giant ears—which might've been bigger than her face—and looked back to the bulletin board. Another flyer stood out to me.

Seeking one working cat. Any sex, species, and coat color welcome.

"I can apply for this one. What's the pay . . ." I ran my eyes over the specific conditions. "This could work."

I nodded to myself then looked at Natsuki. A flyer for a broom-riding job with a witch had already captured her interest. The image of her astride a broom—timid with that bird plushie in her mouth—made me want to burst into laughter, but her motivation was genuine. I had to keep up with her.

"Well then, see you later," I said, turning to leave. But before we completely parted ways, I called over my shoulder, "By the way, the fifth tenet is this: Live every day to the fullest."

Natsuki's eyes widened, sparkling as she watched me.

"Isn't that interesting! You pretended you were sleeping, but you really did listen to the lecturer, Fuuta."

"Well, obviously." I sensed a twitch through my whiskers, and raised my orange tabby tail high. "Anyway, don't work too hard. Pace yourself."

"Yes. We'll live each day to the fullest." She nodded with enthusiasm.

3

"Up two hills, then down one before entering the third intersection," I recited to myself as I walked to the job site, trying to recall the map on the recruitment flyer. This world was loaded with hillside roads. If there were stairs, I'd be able to leap my way up, but all these gradual inclines really wore a cat down.

It'd be a breeze for Michiru's electric bicycle.

Supposedly cats that liked to go places—like me—were rare. Michiru had always put me in a special black carrier and attached me to the basket on her handlebars, where I could enjoy the cool breeze on my face. Every season had its perks. In the spring, the air would be sweet, carrying the strong scent of flowers. In the summer, it would be rich with the smell of warm grass. And in the fall, nature's bright yellow and red leaves would fly around us, flaunting their own kind of beauty. Any cat was bound to become addicted to such outings after experiencing all that just once.

But winter? Well, *obviously* no cat in their right mind would go out on a cold day for fun. Winter days were meant for curling up in front of the heater. That was just common sense.

I must've been deep in thought because a nostalgic scent tickled my nostrils. It smelled like the riverside where Michiru would go cycling. The memory made my vision turn blurry. I swiped my face with my paw.

"Is there a river around here?" I said out loud, stopping to glance at my surroundings, then tilting my head. "Odd. Maybe I was wrong."

I'd passed through two intersections already, but I didn't see a third. Another hill waited ahead of me, but I was certain there'd been a third cross street on that map . . . Not that I'd ever had the best memory.

I went back to the second intersection and loitered around the area. Whiskers came in handy during times like these. They could accurately determine my location and sense even the slightest presence.

A long whisker on my right cheek quivered.

"This way?"

It was no wonder I hadn't noticed it before. Past the corner of the second street was a narrow alleyway just wide enough for a single cat. With my perfect figure, I slipped right through.

"Good thing I didn't eat too many treats," I said to myself, with an internal sigh of relief.

I'd always begged Michiru for my favorite liquid treat, but she'd refuse and tell me I'd only get fat. I'd throw my tantrums, of course, but thanks to her, I stayed in excellent shape. I silently thanked Michiru as I made my way through the alley, which suddenly opened up into a vast space.

"What is this place?" I wondered aloud.

I recalled memories of the park where the neighborhood cats would gather for meetings. It had a slide, two swings, and a sandbox just big enough to fit three kids. Cherry blossom trees would grow between the playground equipment, and when spring came around, the flowers would bloom simultaneously, making the trees look like cotton candy. We cats would use the space at the park's entrance, beneath the treetops, as our meeting spot. Of course, it became harder to attend as I got older, but I was sure they still held meetings there to this day.

This area was about the same size as that park, but in the corner stood an isolated white house. The clearing ended in a sudden decline, where many more houses and cars sat below.

Which world was I standing in right now? This world? Or

that world? I practically felt my eyes twinkle at the sight of it all. At the same time, from where I stood, the land of the living looked so transient.

Only now that I was here did I realize how temporary it really was.

4

A triangular roof topped the white house, and latticed windows graced the face of it on either side of the front door. It could've been plucked straight from a picture book.

As I approached, I noticed a signboard in front. It was an oblong plaque of white-painted plywood, nailed into a wooden post that seemed to sprout from the ground. In the plaque's center, painted in light gray letters, was the business's name: CAFÉ PONT.

"This is the place."

As impressed as I was with my memory and sharp instincts, I had my next steps to think about. The door looked heavy, and required a turned handle to open. If it had been a sliding door, I could've used my claws to drag it open, but doors like this one weren't very cat friendly. It wasn't like I could jump up and turn the handle midair.

My ears perked up in attention, trying to glean some information about what was happening inside. My ears were extremely reliable. Cats had hearing several times better than humans.

But all I could hear inside was the occasional *clink* and *clang* of tableware, and no human voices. From what I could sense, there was only one person inside. I glanced around me, but no one was outside, either. I could wait for a bit, but it didn't seem like anyone would be entering the café anytime soon.

Oh well. I supposed I could try crying.

"Meow." At first I tried a quiet one. Then another one. Then I opened my mouth as wide as it would stretch and put every bit of effort into it. "Meow!"

A *clunk* sounded inside the café. As I wondered what it was, the door opened with a creak. A woman in a white dress stuck her head out. She looked older than Michiru, but younger than Mama. She must've been thirty or forty years old. She glanced around, the long braid down her back wagging like a dog's tail, finally noticing me when she peered at the ground.

"Oh!" she exclaimed. Our eyes met and she beamed.

Us cats could understand human words, but we didn't have the easiest time translating our language to them. I tried, anyway.

"I saw your help-wanted flyer," I started.

My words must've been crystal clear because she replied easily.

"A newbie, huh? Come on in," she said with a welcoming gesture.

I followed her in, surveilling the inside and wondering *what* exactly this person could possibly be, if she understood me so easily.

"Oh dear. Do you think I'm some sort of ghost?" she asked. "I'm not a ghost, nor any other monstrous thing, for that matter. I'm a real-life human, through and through. Look." She lifted the hem of her long dress and exposed her feet. "See? I have legs."

"But how?" I asked.

"You mean, how do I understand you? I act as an intermediary between this world and that world. If I couldn't speak to the cats who work with me, then we'd never get anything done," she answered with a shrug.

"Which world does this café exist in?" I asked.

"This world, that world . . . it's one of those things. From that world's perspective, it's that . . . Argh! I'm confusing myself." She gripped her braided hair and contorted her face in frustration. "We mostly operate on one side. To put it more simply, we operate in the living world's present day. Our customers come from there."

"I have a suggestion," I offered, still a little mixed up in my head. I let every hair on my body puff up with a flair that I channeled into my statement.

"And what's that?" she asked.

"Saying *this* world and *that* world gets confusing. Why don't we rename them? Maybe First World or Second World, for example. Or Beginner Level or Advanced Level."

I lived a full lifespan in the other world before I came here. I liked the idea of a name that indicated a "step up," but she only hummed in dissatisfaction. After some thought, she gave an alternate suggestion.

"How about colors?" she offered. "Blue for the afterlife, and green for the land of the living. We can call them 'the land of blue' and 'the land of green.'"

Blue was the color of sky and sea. Green was the color of land and forests. Both were sparkling seasonal colors.

"I like it," I said.

She nodded firmly in approval. "I'm Nijiko, the café's owner. I take requests from the people of this . . . er, from the land of green. Cats from the land of blue then grant those requests. You could say I'm the middleman."

It sounded like she was similar to a hostess or liaison in charge of running a geisha house. But I still had a hard time wrapping my whiskers around it. One thing was clear, though: The cats' job was to follow her instructions.

"I'm Fuuta. Nice to meet you," I responded. It was best to start off with a humble introduction. I could figure out the rest while we talked. "Is it true that completing five tasks earns a cat a special reward?"

Reading that detail on the flyer was what had motivated me to come here.

"Of course. If you complete five tasks' worth of work, you won't be required to wait the standard seven months before you can cross into the land of green to see your loved ones. In fact, some cats get it done in about four months, if they hustle. Make sure you work hard, too, okay?"

Nijiko might as well have offered me catnip. "Leave it to me."

"Other cats, however, lounge around all day and let seven months pass without completing any of the five tasks."

That drove the point home for me. If I didn't *hustle*, there'd be no purpose to my work here.

Somehow, I felt energized. I leaped up to the top of a bookshelf that was nestled against the wall. "Keep the work coming, then."

"Pace yourself," Nijiko warned. "If you don't do it right, it won't count."

I sat proudly atop the bookshelf, my paws positioned firmly on the edge. She leveled her gaze at me. She seemed like she'd be pretty strict. Still, she allowed me to stay where I was as she began to explain the job in detail.

The bookshelf gave me a full view of the café. There were three tables for customers. Each one had two fabric-covered chairs. The coarseness of the fabric made them perfect scratching posts. On the wall opposite of this bookshelf sat a wood fireplace. The brick mantel made the space feel like it belonged in a fairy tale. Knickknacks from foreign countries decorated the top. The café's interior was overall rather spacious, about the size of the living-and-dining area of Michiru's house, where she'd even kept the TV.

The kitchen, though, was much smaller than Michiru's. It had only a single-burner stovetop next to the sink, plus a rolling kitchen wagon that served dual functions as a worktable and storage space. Michiru's refrigerator had seven doors and reached the ceiling (with just enough space for me to squeeze into, of course), but the one in this kitchen had only two doors. Not to mention it was only as tall as Nijiko's waistline.

She'd called this place a café, but I couldn't imagine it served anything special. After all, Mama and Papa were amazing cooks, and their kitchen clearly reflected that. Mama could take one peek into the refrigerator and make all kinds of dishes. And on weekends, I'd find Papa in the kitchen, where he'd be making rillettes, confit, and all kinds of fancy foreign treats. Those were the days in which Papa and Mama would pop open a wine bottle—Michiru would have soda, and I would have water—and enjoy one another's company.

"Hey. Are you listening?" Nijiko said, drawing me back to the present.

Thinking about wine must've made me zone out.

"Look at this. This is the letterbox in question," she said as she lifted a box on top of a dresser that served as a divider between the kitchen and customer seating area.

Atop the bookshelf, I felt the warmth rise from the fireplace. In the land of green, early summer might've been the most pleasant time of year for most people, but cats knew that the happiest of places were the ones that were warm year-round. Even the hottest summers could get cold at night in a way that humans would never understand. It's why house cats often curled up on our humans' laps or snuggled up against their chests.

As much as I wanted to bask in the warmth of the flames below, I knew the drowsiness would catch up to me in no time. I hopped down to the floor.

According to Nijiko's explanation, the café's main service was to arrange meetings between people. The way it worked was simple. A customer would write the name of the person they wished to see on a special card and place it inside the café's letterbox. That was where Nijiko as the café owner stepped in. She would use her various methods to identify and locate the target in question, but it was the messenger cat's job to bring the customer and recipient together.

"But you *won't* be bringing anyone with you in person," she explained. "Think about it. If you had to escort someone dead—in other words, someone from the land of blue—you'd have to resurrect them first. That's not our place."

Apparently there *were* figures within the land of blue who dealt with resurrection. I licked my mouth and glanced around me, impressed with how many different occupations there were in the afterlife.

"Then how do I bring people together?" I asked, impatient for answers. I flashed one of my canines in a threatening manner, but Nijiko barely reacted. In fact, the gesture made her look fatigued.

"You find out what the target wants to say to the client, then deliver only their soul," she replied.

The way she put it made it sound like I was supposed to use the soul to possess a stranger, who would speak the message on the target's behalf.

"That reminds me of a legend . . . something about Mount Osore . . ." I pondered.

When Michiru had been in middle school, the mythology surrounding Mount Osore—a mountain that served as a supposed gate to the underworld—had become a big topic. She'd told Mama about it, saying there were stories about souls of the dead possessing people's bodies and speaking messages from beyond.

Nijiko furrowed her brow. "Are you talking about a medium?" she asked.

"Yeah, that. That's the exact word I remember."

When Michiru had said the word *medium*, I'd first thought she was talking about the size of an animal, or maybe even a type of fish. But then it sounded like *medium* referred to a job that women performed at a place called Mount Osore, in the northeast of Japan, where they relayed messages from the dead.

"Mediums and messenger cats are completely different," Nijiko said, shaking her head. "Messenger cats meet the deceased speaker in person. They put time and effort into forming a connection between people. Not that I know how mediums connect with the dead."

Nijiko shrugged and then gave me a wink. I could've sworn I saw a twinkle in her eye. A moment later, I let out a big sneeze. My instincts were suddenly on edge, but I couldn't put my paw on why exactly.

"Anyway, step one is to practice. You'll learn by doing, okay?"

She was right. There was no point in getting worked up about mistakes I hadn't made yet. Frankly I couldn't understand how humans upset themselves like that. I wished they would've watched and learned from us cats once in a while. We were masters at adapting to the moment.

I extended my front paws and stretched my back into a deep arch, my signal that I was ready for action.

"This is the task chart. I wrote your name here," Nijiko explained, brandishing in front of me a small paper with a flap. Each messenger cat in the café was named in a tidy list, but only a few seemed to be doing real work. They had varying numbers of pawprint stamps next to their names.

"One completed task earns one pawprint stamp," Nijiko explained. She slipped the task chart into the clipboard that dangled from the dresser. It closed with a *snap*.

So five of these stamps would earn me the reward. Watching the clipboard swing gave me a burst of motivation. In fact, I wanted to sprint around the café in a fit of zoomies. But there were lots of breakables in here, and I didn't want to cause any trouble, so I stayed put.

"I'll be counting on you, messenger cat," Nijiko said.

I'd only come for an interview, but now Nijiko offered me a treat that came in a long, narrow package. It was my favorite liquid treat.

"You're a nice person," I replied.

What could I say? I was easy to please.

By the time I left the café, the full moon was shining. Ever since arriving in the land of blue, the moon had looked stunning. I retraced my steps back through the narrow alleyway, and I hoped Michiru was looking at the same moon that I was.

5

Messenger cats didn't have clock-in or clock-out times. We were allowed to come to Café Pont at our leisure. However, we weren't allowed to enter the café between the operating hours of ten A.M. to five P.M. It would startle the customers if we wandered around inside.

"I'm not running a cat café, you know," Nijiko had huffed when she'd explained it to me.

I was fully nocturnal (most cats were), so I usually slept until the afternoon. Today was no different. It was evening by the time I felt like setting out. Once I reached Café Pont, Nijiko was hanging the CLOSED sign.

"Hey," I called.

"Oh, Fuuta. Welcome. You're early."

"I wanted to get used to the routine quickly," I said, hoping to show a newcomer's enthusiasm.

It wasn't good for anyone to do nothing but loaf in this world. After all, the body needed to move to stay nimble. And walking up and down the hills *was* good exercise.

"I was just about to open the letterbox," she said, finishing up at the door. "Want to take a look with me?"

I followed Nijiko inside, then stepped behind the dresser upon which the letterbox sat. She inserted a retro-style key into the keyhole, turned it with a click, and opened the lid. I peered into the box, where around twenty postcard-sized folded cards sat. The customer's name was written on the front of each card. On the back was the name of the person they wanted to see. Inside, they'd written out lengthy, heartfelt messages, as if they'd penned a letter they expected the recipient to read. Some of them were even decorated with drawings and stickers.

Nijiko deftly sorted through them, checking both sides of each card.

"Something like this one isn't feasible," she explained, showing me the back of one card. It had the name of a member of a famous five-member dance group that even *I* knew about.

"Why would someone write *that*?" I asked. Then again, the person was a celebrity. It made sense that people would want to meet them.

"Famous people are a big hassle. They involve permissions and agencies and other hoops to jump through."

Our operations were strictly kept a secret from our targets, so if the truth of our job ever did leak, it'd only cause issues later on.

"This kind of request isn't doable, either," she added. The next letter came with a name and drawing of a commander from the Warring States period. It was so detailed that I nearly mistook it for a photo. "Anything a historical figure says could change history itself, right?"

That made sense.

Nijiko leafed through a few more cards and shared how she'd manage them. Then her hand paused. She considered the handwriting on the one she held.

She offered it to me. "Would you like to try this one?"

"Ooh," I marveled, eager for my first task.

The cursive was written with a ballpoint pen. The light strokes looked mature and developed. The letters were placed neatly in the center.

I want to see my late father.

The client's name was written on the back: *Yuzu Minami.*

How in the world was I supposed to glean anything about Yuzu's father based on this little information? My whiskers twitched, then Nijiko decided to throw me a fish.

"The card was submitted this afternoon . . . Ah, I remember. Two women nearing forty or so came by," she recalled.

Nijiko then closed her eyes and recounted the events.

One woman had said, "Yuzu, first of all, congratulations on completing your book. Now all that's left is to wait for bookstores to shelve it."

"It's thanks to your support, Isobe," Yuzu replied. "I still can't believe I'm going to receive an award, and that my artwork is being turned into a book."

One woman—Yuzu—wore a thin blouse with embroidery on it. The younger woman—Isobe—wore a sharp gray suit. They didn't quite interact the way normal work colleagues would, but based on the conversation, their relationship became clear. Isobe was Yuzu's editor.

Apparently, Yuzu had ordered a soy milk tea. Isobe had ordered a hot coffee. Nijiko made a point to mention that she boiled soy milk and black tea leaves in a small saucepan to create a rich flavor in her milk teas.

She continued recounting the story.

Isobe asked, "Are the exhibition preparations proceeding well?"

"The framing is finished, but smaller tasks like creating title labels and printing the profiles are keeping me busy," Yuzu replied.

"I imagine so. There's just one week left. I'll be there to help once it's time to carry the frames inside."

"That'll help a lot. Thank you."

"Remind me, is the venue close to the station?"

Yuzu answered with the name of the station, Isuzu Station. "Once you exit the ticket gate it'll lead directly to a strip mall. There's a sweets shop in the middle of it. The gallery is above it, on the second floor. It's only about a two- or three-minute walk from the station."

"Then it shouldn't be too much trouble, even with our arms full. Let me know if anything comes up."

They'd only come to the café for a short while—less than an hour—but it sounded like they'd been ready to leave.

I placed a paw on the piece of paper in front of me. "So, this is the card Yuzu put inside the letterbox?"

On the dresser, next to the old wooden letterbox (which was more like a square box with a sad little slit in it), was a felt pen and papers yellowed with age. The papers read, *Survey: Who do you wish to meet?* The letters weren't exactly easy to read. They looked like wiggly worms. Not real ones, though. Real ones were chubby and squirmy and . . . oops. Just thinking about worms had me subconsciously extending my paw, directly into the path of a flower vase.

Luckily I didn't knock it over. I breathed a sigh of relief. If it had fallen and water had spilled out, I could've gotten soaked. Just imagining that made me shudder. In fact, even though I didn't have a drop on me, the thought made me concerned enough to check the side of my body and lick it. Only then did I calm down.

"Do you understand the gist?" Nijiko asked.

"Basically, Yuzu Minami is an artist whose work will be displayed at an exhibition soon," I summarized.

"I'd say that sums it up."

Nijiko didn't sound surprised. I pushed on. "So she wants her late father to see her exhibition."

My tail stood pin straight.

"She *did* explicitly say that," Nijiko remarked.

I flashed my canines in protest. She'd been trying to say that this whole time? She ignored me and continued on to the part of the story where the two women readied themselves to leave.

At the register, Isobe moved to pay for both of them.

"This is considered a meeting, so it'll be categorized as an expense," she said to Yuzu, who ducked her head in appreciation. That's when Yuzu noticed the letterbox next to the register.

"What is that box for?" she asked.

"It's not a mere box. It's a letterbox," Nijiko amended. "If you write the name of the person you wish to see and place it inside this box, you might get to see them."

The two women exchanged glances.

"However, seeing *them takes a different meaning here,*" she went on. "*If they come to you, they might take a different form. They won't speak their name or confirm who they are. You'll only receive a flicker of a feeling, where you'll wonder if it was them. Do you accept?*"

"Hold it right there," I interrupted. "Appearing in a different form is one thing, but if the target can't identify themselves, how is the customer supposed to know it was them? Do we tell them ahead of time?"

She shook her head. "We don't do anything like that. But the customer will know. You'll choose words or phrases from the target, something the customer would recognize as distinct to their target, and deliver them. If they don't recognize the words, that either means the correct words weren't chosen or the recipient wasn't receptive to them, which would essentially render the 'meeting' meaningless. As if it never happened," she huffed.

"*I'm* supposed to choose the words? You won't do that part for me, too?"

Nijiko wagged a finger at my face.

"That's *your* job, messenger cat. You're the ones who actually go to meet each person. Only someone who has met the individuals can pick out the right words to deliver. Don't you agree?"

There was only one answer to that.

"I guess so." I pushed down my flustered feelings and continued. "So it's up to the messenger cat to ensure the client *feels* like they encountered that person?"

As much as I trembled under the weight of this responsibility, Nijiko smiled warmly and nodded. She then continued her story.

The caveat was out in the open. Isobe's eyes sparkled.

"Since we're here, let's write something," she suggested.

Yuzu nodded strongly to the invitation. They hurried back to their seats, where they each turned their focus to a card.

"Now that I'm actually doing it, it's hard to pick someone," Isobe admitted.

While she hesitated, Yuzu's pen flew across the card, as if she'd decided a long time ago whose name she would write. Once they both finished, they showed each other their cards.

"Oh that's lovely." Isobe's stare softened as she looked at Yuzu's card. "It'd be nice if your father could see your exhibition."

Yuzu beamed.

"By the way, what did the editor Isobe write?" I asked.

I flipped over her card. She'd written, *My future husband.* Boy, did the secondhand embarrassment shudder through me.

"Do you grant requests like this, too?" I marveled.

"Of course not. People need to find someone to marry on their own," she retorted. "I'm busy here, and it's not like I have an army of messenger cats. That's why I only grant the wishes of people who are most distressed or unable to see the person they want to see."

If that was her metric, then this request fit as perfectly as a cat could inside a box.

"We can't handle everything," she reminded me. Her tone took on weight. "Imagination is very important for this job. You need to work on yours."

6

The next day, I buckled down and got to work.

As much as I disliked waking up early, if I didn't align my waking hours with those of humans, I'd never be able to do my job. Or at least that had been my intention. I was out cold until evening.

"Oh rats!" I yelped and leaped to my paws. But panicking never got a job done well. Instead, I took a long time to stretch and groom, which wasted more time. I ended up in a mad dash to get to work.

I thought about greeting Nijiko beforehand, but if she ended up nagging me for starting work so late, that would make getting future tasks more difficult. Boy, did I make this hard on myself.

Careful to keep my footfalls silent, I slipped past the café. The entrance to the land of green waited just beyond it.

Before now, I'd thought this was merely another road on a hill, but a long bridge of sorts stood on the other side by which an attendant waited: a male cat with a brown and black coat—a tortoiseshell cat, in other words. He intimidated me with a sharp glance, but he was probably on the job, too.

"Travel permit," he said flatly.

How demanding.

I flashed the paper Nijiko had given me yesterday. It noted my destination—Isuzu Station—and featured her special cat stamp. The tortoiseshell harrumphed as he studied my travel permit.

"You're a messenger cat?" he asked, his face leaning brazenly into mine.

"So what if I am?" I countered. "It's my first task. That's something to celebrate."

We were both male cats. My jolt of pride quickly spiraled into a near impulse for a catfight.

"Fine," he dissented, then stepped aside to let me cross.

Before I knew it, I had arrived at Isuzu Station. I stood in front of the sign beneath the station's roof, where the name was displayed in big letters. I didn't understand how the travel system worked, but it seemed to me that there was some sort of oversight method that dictated crossings between the land of green and the land of blue.

Now that I was in the land of green, my first thought was to try to see Michiru again. But the complexity of the travel system made it impossible.

"Once I finish my five tasks, I can go see her fair and square," I encouraged myself, and started walking.

I would start my task by investigating my client. I'd chosen Isuzu Station because there hadn't been any other notable locations from the clues I had. All I *did* know was that Yuzu Minami would hold an exhibition at a gallery in the Isuzu Station strip mall next week. She'd be busy with the preparations right about now.

"Imagination is harder to use than I thought," I mumbled.

I walked through the strip mall, and looked left and right, remembering how Nijiko had told me I need to improve my imagination. I spotted a carefree cat curled up on the side of the street, but the cat didn't appear to be part of my new world. It glanced at me, but didn't react. I supposed it didn't notice the difference between us.

The strip mall contained all kinds of shops: a bakery, produce store, drugstore . . . and more. People bustled their way home from work. Then, the most wonderful scent lured me to a seafood counter, where fresh fish lined the display. I wouldn't receive any pay for a while, and I didn't have time to buy and eat a snack. I gave up on the fish and hurried along.

A poster in front of a flower shop flapped and rustled in the breeze. I brushed past other equally tempting things, like flowers wrapped in cellophane, until I finally reached a lone sweets shop. It was an old-fashioned store; the window boasted ohagi—rice balls covered with red bean paste—and skewered glazed dango. Rows of steamed buns, too. The glass window on the door had a poster attached to it that read, GALLERY DIRECTIONS, with instructions on how to attend the exhibition next week.

"This is the place," I declared.

It was an old three-story building. The gallery occupied the second floor. The sweets shop had a staircase inside of it that led directly to the gallery, but the building's main staircase—outside—led to a back entrance on the second floor.

Using the main staircase, I dashed upstairs and found the back door cracked open. I peered through, into a vast, empty white space. Not a single object occupied the walls or floor.

Is no one here? I wondered.

Just as I was about to step inside, the sound of someone ascending the outdoor staircase rose from below. I slunk away to the corner of the landing to hide. A petite woman with two heavy paper bags in her arms brushed past me and entered the room. The moment she did, a second woman's voice came from inside. She must've used the indoor staircase to enter the gallery.

I directed my ears toward the conversation. My ears could pick up sounds from long distances. I'd always been convinced that this was thanks to their fantastically pointed shape, but even cats with the droopiest ears could hear faraway noises.

"I'll be helping you next week," the first woman said, the sound of paper bags thumping against the floor accompanying her.

"Hello, Ms. Minami. We've been expecting you."

The woman who came up the main set of stairs must be Yuzu Minami, then. In that case, the other woman must be someone affiliated with the gallery.

"The framed paintings will be here in two days, but I took you up on your offer to bring some things early," Yuzu said.

If she was scheduled to bring her art to the gallery in two days, that meant her editor, Isobe—the woman who'd been at the café with her—would be here to help then, too.

"Yes, please do," the second woman replied. "Our previous exhibition ended on Monday. I contacted you thinking earlier preparation might help."

Interested, I snuck toward the back door for a peek through the crack. The gallery woman had gray hair that was pulled up into a bun. Yuzu smiled politely at her. I'd imagined an artist would have a stereotypically "unique" appearance, but Yuzu seemed comparatively plain.

"Thank you," she replied. "This is my first exhibition, so I'm unfamiliar with how things go. I'll do what I can to avoid any problems for you."

She cast her eyes down. She must've been nervous, but this level of shyness practically begged for placating words.

From their conversation, I gathered that Yuzu had an exhibition meeting and a preliminary setup after this. I retreated to my corner space on the landing and waited on standby.

I thought back to what Yuzu had looked like just now. Her rounded shoulders made her look much shorter than she actually was. I knew all about rounded postures like that—cats hunched their backs, too—but even cats didn't do it all the time like she seemed to. I decided to camp out on the landing where no one could see me, and lay on my belly, my legs splayed out in front and behind me.

I only looked up when I heard the sound of the back door opening. I'd fit so perfectly into this little space that I'd nodded off for a bit. I hurried onto my paws, shook out my body to fully wake up, then followed Yuzu down the stairs. We returned to the strip mall, and then the station. Was she about to board the train?

Now that I thought about it, Nijiko *did* say it was okay for me to ride the trains if it helped my pursuit—but anything from having my picture taken to being petted could slow me down and get me in real trouble. Just one brief interaction had the potential to snowball into something bigger. There were times when I was alive that I'd picked the wrong park for a stroll and found myself surrounded by children within seconds. I needed to be careful, and make sure people turned a blind eye to my presence.

Nervousness shot through me. This would be my very first time on a train; I hadn't even been on one when I was alive.

Just as I was about to slip under the ticket gate, Yuzu's phone rang.

"Yuzu?" asked the caller.

I held my ears to cling to the voice on the other end of the line. It wasn't hard to hear phone conversations. I could even tell that the speaker was an elderly woman.

"Hi, Mom. What is it?" Yuzu replied with a sigh. She turned her back on the ticket gate as if she was about to leave the station, but then she started walking a path parallel to the railway track. She must've expected the phone call to last a while if she intended to walk home instead of disturbing the other passengers. Based on how easily she made the decision, this must've been a pattern.

"It's about your father's memorial service," her mother said.

The roadside flowers had snagged my attention—but that comment made my whiskers twitch.

"Yeah. It's in November, right?" Yuzu replied.

November was five months away. Well, mothers were often quick to make decisions.

"I want to make preparations early," her mother said. "Will you come the day before? Your brother can't come until the day of because Kinako has school."

"I don't know if I can this far in advance, but I *would* like to go early."

"Okay." The mother's tone shifted, as if she was relieved. "I'm thinking about limiting it to immediate family only. After the sutras are spoken, we can have lunch at the hotel. I hear they have traditional five-course bento boxes."

"That sounds good, right? Want me to make reservations?"

"No, no. Your father's old friends run the place, so I'll ask them myself."

With that conversation at a halt, Yuzu steeled herself to speak.

"Um, hey," she started.

The response was laced with expectation. "What is it? Did something good happen?"

"I'm publishing an art book. It's going to receive an award."

"Wow, really? Congratulations."

But the words didn't seem to make Yuzu happy. Even the enthusiasm on the other end seemed to wither.

"I thought maybe you'd met someone special," her mother admitted. "I suppose I assumed wrong."

"That's never going to happen," Yuzu said sharply.

"Listen, Yuzu. You can't give up on love. You have a long

life ahead of you. I was with your father for almost fifty years, and we had a happy run. It's okay to work hard, but if you don't work on your relationships, I know your father will worry in the afterlife."

I doubted most of what she'd said had reached Yuzu, since she'd pulled the phone away from her ear about halfway through the conversation and kept walking. And once she hung up, Yuzu stuffed the phone into her bag. Her steps hastened, as if she wanted to leave her mother's words in the dust.

After a thirty-minute walk, she reached another three-story apartment building. From the outside, I watched a light turn on in the second room of the first floor. That must've been Yuzu's apartment. I jumped on top of the hedges to peer through her curtain. She didn't change out of her clothes before flopping onto the bed. She must've been tired.

"I guess this is all the information I can gather for today," I told myself.

Just as I was about to leave, Yuzu practically leaped off the bed and walked to her dresser, where she withdrew a large A4-sized envelope. It looked old and yellowed; it was stuffed with papers. Yuzu stared at it for a few moments, but didn't withdraw anything before she ultimately slid it back in the drawer.

7

The next day, I dropped by Café Pont to report on what I'd learned. It was generally best to deliver information while it was still fresh. Time tended to whittle down the finer details of my memory.

"I see," Nijiko replied as she washed the dishes.

"Now I want to go talk to her father. How am I supposed to find him?" I asked.

She looked up from her task. "Her father is here, in the land of blue, right? You can use his name to find his address."

"His name?"

"Yes. His alias in the land of blue."

Nijiko explained that when people died, they received a name to use in the land of blue. It was similar to a code name. Saying it allowed the listener to instantly piece together where they lived and what kinds of hobbies they had, so it was a great way for people to get to know one another. But that alias didn't convey the name they'd used in the land of green.

"I can look it up," she said. "His last name was Minami, right? If you have his age at his time of death and the month he died, that should be enough information."

Nijiko went to the dresser and opened up a laptop—which frankly didn't match the whole vibe of this café. Considering that the travel permits were made of paper, I was surprised to see that digital technology was involved. But I supposed if there was a citizen registry of sorts, it had to be searchable.

"They mentioned a memorial service for him in November," I said, recalling the information I'd gathered.

"A Buddhist memorial? That could mark the second, sixth, or even twelfth anniversary of his death."

"They didn't say which one. They *did* mention it would be for immediate family only, and that they would eat lunch at the hotel."

"Immediate family only? Then the second anniversary is probably off the table."

After all, a second-anniversary Buddhist memorial service wouldn't be hosted at the same scope as the initial funeral, but there'd still be a lot of people. But if only immediate family were planning to attend this one, then a sixth- or twelfth-anniversary service—the next two anniversaries that would be observed—made more sense. Of course, it was technically possible that they'd made arrangements for an even later anniversary, but based on the conversation, he hadn't died *that* long ago.

"There was another clue," I realized.

I explained how Yuzu's mother had mentioned that she and her husband had been together for nearly fifty years. Considering the age he must've reached for that to be true—alongside the scope of the service—my best guess was that he'd been dead for six years.

"Great. Let's use that information to look him up," Nijiko replied.

She typed away at her laptop.

"Found it! This must be him, right? Shouichi Minami. Age at death: Seventy-two." Just in case, she looked up whether he had died in November two or twelve years ago. "I don't see anyone else with the surname 'Minami' that meets these conditions."

Lucky for us, his surname was spelled with rare Kanji characters. Nijiko jotted down the search result—his alias for the land of blue—and handed it to me.

"This is a long name," I observed, running my gaze over a lengthy string of characters.

"The first three characters denote his address."

The alias even indicated his hobbies and life's achievements in the land of green. I supposed there was a point to having such a long name. I purred lightly, the sound vibrating deep in my throat.

"Here. I'll give you a treat," Nijiko said.

I hadn't done this investigation for a treat, but I'd take what I could get.

Three sardines later, I left Café Pont.

8

Up three hills, then down two, I found the address I was looking for.

Several small, stylish dwellings were lined up to form a single village. Rather than independent homes, the whole village had open-door access. People milled about everywhere, engaged in their own activities. The tranquil atmosphere was a little different from where "trainees" like me currently dwelled.

A man sat on a bench. He was writing something. Maybe poetry, or even a haiku.

"Excuse me," I called out to him.

"Oh? Are you a messenger cat?"

I nodded. "Yes."

His eyes sparkled. "Are you here to see me?"

"Um, what's your name . . . ?"

His answer suggested he wasn't Yuzu's father.

"Tsk. Here I thought my wife wanted to see me enough to request contact from a messenger cat," he muttered.

Poor guy.

"You're done with your afterlife training," I pointed out. "Can't you go see her whenever you want?"

I didn't know how things worked for humans in this world, but my guess couldn't have been far off.

"Well, that would be the logical answer," he replied. "But without a solid reason, I can't cross back and forth all willy-nilly. There's the 'balance' to consider, you know?"

So it *wasn't* an exaggeration when they said the shape of the earth could warp.

"I can go during the Obon festival, but otherwise the procedure is a lot to deal with. That's why I've been waiting for a messenger cat. A request would allow me to go immediately. But . . ."

Messenger cats couldn't do anything unless a request came from the other world. Put in other terms, unless someone from the land of green wanted to see *him*, our paws were tied.

The man's shoulders slumped. As bad as I felt for him, I had a job to do.

"I'm searching for this person." I handed him a piece of paper with the name Nijiko had written down for me.

He pointed. "See that man over there with the camera?

That's him. A lot of art enthusiasts dwell in this district, but he's got a particularly good eye."

I glanced over my shoulder to see who he'd pointed at: a man clad in denim. Yuzu's father had died in his seventies, but the man taking photos appeared to be in his forties. In this world, he didn't appear elderly. Individuals chose the age in which they wanted to appear.

Now that I thought about it, my coat had become glossier since I'd come here. Even my appetite had returned, as hearty as it was in my youth. No one had explicitly asked me to choose my preferred age, but my body felt healthy. I swished my tail with vigor as I approached the man in denim.

"Hello. Nice to meet you. I'm Fuuta, a messenger cat."

Shouichi's eyes widened. "That's a long tail you're slinging around," he joked.

"Your daughter, Yuzu, made a request, so I came to see you."

His expression fell. "Yeah. I watch her frequently from here. I have a good idea of how she's been."

I followed his gaze. Ah—I saw what he meant. This location offered a decent view of the land of green. I strained my eyes to see if I could catch a glimpse of Michiru, but as I expected, it seemed difficult to spot her.

He smiled while I relayed how his daughter had been.

"I was just brewing some tea. Would you like some?" he

offered. "I know you won't want anything hot, so I'll cool it down for you."

We entered his warm living room, where he offered me a small bowl. A sweet scent wafted up from it, filling the space. I lapped at the tea, but the slight bitterness made me scrunch up my face.

"Sorry, that's my fault," he said, quickly rushing to the fridge. He poured a dash of milk into the bowl to make milk tea instead.

"This reminds me," I began, "Yuzu had ordered soy milk tea at the café."

I told him everything Nijiko had told me about Yuzu's visit.

"Yuzu and I have similar taste," he explained. "Not just in food and drinks, but our hobbies, too. See my camera?"

I glanced at where he'd set his camera beside him.

His eyes narrowed as if sinking into a memory. "She's an artist, so we often spent time outside together. I'd take photos while she sketched beside me."

"Well, now she's about to open an exhibition. She's going to receive an award, *and* her work will be published in an art book."

"She's hosting an exhibition," he echoed, nodding as if deeply moved. "How about that. I wish I could be there in person, but that's not the way it goes. I've got a lot going on here, too."

His daughter had his eyes. If only she would smile like he did, she'd look cute.

"Give her lots of praise for me!" he said as I gathered myself to leave.

He waved after me until I couldn't see him anymore.

9

Today was the day I was going to deliver the message. My body shook, but not from nervousness. I trembled with excitement.

"Strike while the iron's hot," Nijiko had told me, with the gesture to match, by way of a send-off.

I arrived at the foot of the bridge, and the same tortoiseshell cat from before stood guard.

"Hey, newbie. How's the job going?" he asked.

Shameless attitude, as usual.

"I'm about to deliver the message," I told him, moving past him to cross the bridge.

"Hey," he yelled. The way he called out to me sounded threatening. Did he still want something? But when I turned to face him, he added, "Good luck. Make sure they meet."

He grinned with his teeth. Gee, he was surprisingly charming.

"I will. Leave it to me," I said, tail in the air, and strutted across the bridge.

Once I arrived at Isuzu Station, I waited patiently for Yuzu. Right on schedule, she exited through the ticket gate. I followed her at once.

Today marked the fifth day of her ten-day exhibition. As soon as she entered the gallery, I waited on the side of the sweets shop, observing the influx of people.

I held on tight to Yuzu's father's soul inside of me. When cats feel excited or threatened, our tails puff up several times their normal size. Emotion and shock could make it puff up instinctively, but we could do it at will, as well. Nijiko had told me that messenger cats would use this mechanism to imbue the souls into a person we chose to deliver the message.

I strained my body and pushed his soul into my tail. I'd already practiced moving it back and forth, so I managed to do it perfectly. But I couldn't find the most vital piece of my mission: a person into which to transfer the soul.

"There's a surprising lack of suitable carriers," I mumbled, looking around me.

It wasn't that there weren't enough people around. This was a strip mall, after all, and it had the typical foot traffic that came with one. But based on how quickly they walked, so many people looked too busy. Many were families with children. None of them would've made good messengers.

"Well, I have some time . . ." Just as I thought I'd curl up on the ground, the sound of footsteps closed in on the shop. It was a woman in a pantsuit. She stopped right in front of the entrance and opened the sweets shop's glass-window door.

"Is Yuzu here yet?" she called.

"Yes, she's on the second floor," came the saleswoman's voice.

The suit-wearing lady proceeded toward the stairs, where she made her way up to the gallery.

From where I sat, I couldn't expect to hear the voices on the second floor. I took the outside staircase and investigated from the back entrance.

"Working hard?" asked the suit-wearing lady.

"Oh, hello, Isobe," Yuzu answered, turning toward her.

Now I understood. The suit-wearing lady was Yuzu's editor, Isobe. I was glad I hadn't yet chosen a soul carrier. Isobe was the perfect fit if I could find a way to get closer to her.

Here I thought the choosing process would get tricky. I clearly had a great eye for this.

The conversation continued. "The editor in chief told me you've had a lot of visitors."

"Thanks to you. And thank you again for your help moving the frames inside," Yuzu replied, modest as always.

"Do you think you'll be okay for the award ceremony tonight?" Isobe asked.

Huh? The award ceremony was tonight? I had no idea. I strained my ears to hear more.

"Yes. I plan to go after a pit stop at home."

"Sorry to spring it on you in the middle of the exhibition. The venue couldn't host it any other day," Isobe said apologetically.

So the jig was up tonight? This was no time to loaf around for a catnap. Time was of the essence. I leaped over five steps and onto the ground. The second I landed, a businessman in his fifties or so passed by. He stopped in front of the sweets shop for a glimpse at a poster advertising the gallery.

"Change of plans. That's my messenger," I said, determined.

I sidled up beside him as naturally as possible and focused my power into the tip of my tail. Now that it had taken a concentrated form, the soul tingled. Just as I puffed up my tail, I slid the tip toward the man's leg. Yuzu's father's soul would transfer into his body for only a short period of time.

A small boy ran between us, just close enough to brush my tail first.

Uh-oh.

It was too late. I couldn't stop it. The boy's leg had already touched my tail, which meant I'd made a real scratching post of my very first job. I hung my head in shame. I had failed, even after Nijiko warned me to be extra careful about not touching the wrong person.

"Souls can also transfer into objects, not just people," she'd explained. "You need to be extra vigilant once you puff up your tail."

"Well, obviously I'll be vigilant. If I touch a telephone pole or something, it won't speak the message for me," I'd said and laughed wryly.

I wanted to tell my past self to take her warning more seriously and *be careful*, but I'd already clawed all these days of hard work to shreds. I sat disgruntled over the fact that I wouldn't receive a stamp today.

The boy, unaware of my sulking, entered the sweets shop as he shouted, "Mom!"

A woman who'd just bought some sweets turned to look at him. "Oh, Yohito. I told you to wait with your grandma."

That very grandma stood in front of the shop, chatting with another woman. The boy took this moment to slip away into the staircase at the back.

His mother panicked. "Hey! Yohito! You can't go up there."

"It's fine. There's a display in the art gallery on the second floor," the shopkeeper warmly told the boy. "Go have a look."

How in the world would this unfold? I went around the back and made my way up the outdoor staircase, then stood on standby near the back entrance. Just then, Yuzu turned her proud yet soft gaze on the boy.

"What a cute guest you are," she remarked. "Take your time to look around."

No one else but the two of them were inside. Isobe must've left at some point. The boy loitered timidly at first, but his eyes quickly took on a new light as he gazed at all the artwork.

"I like this one!" he exclaimed, stopping in his tracks to admire one in particular. He glanced up at Yuzu who'd been following him.

She smiled. "Really? Thank you. This painting is of the lotus field I used to visit with my father when I was a child."

Just as I started to wonder if she'd ever mentioned that fact before, Yohito shaped a rectangle out of his pointer fingers and thumbs. He held it to his eye and whispered, "Click."

Yuzu's eyes widened in surprise, as if recognizing the gesture. She then turned her eyes downward, happiness flooding into them. Her soft, hooded gaze resembled her father's.

Yuzu remained quiet as she followed Yohito through his viewing. Piece by piece, he took in each painting, then smiled one final time.

"You did a good job," he told her.

They stood in front of the painting on the farthest wall of the room. I couldn't see their expressions from where I was hidden, but I got the sense that Yuzu's shoulders trembled slightly.

Her reply was just short of a whisper. "Thank you for viewing them."

"A lot of stuff happened, but you're at your happiest now, right? And you sought it out yourself. You should be proud."

Yuzu nodded, pride coloring her expression.

"Yohito, we're leaving!" his mother called from downstairs.

He hurried back to the stairs. Yuzu watched him leave, the sound of his footsteps pitter-pattering all the way down, then bent over to pick something up from the floor. Although I'd only got a view from the side, I could tell she was smiling. Once she straightened, the object in her hand angled to where I could see it, too.

It was a photograph.

The photo displayed a vibrant lotus field, as far as the eye could see. I hadn't brought that photo. Maybe someone else had brought it—or maybe her father had snuck it through himself, knowing I'd be here. Whether he did or not didn't matter, though.

Balance between the worlds was preserved.

Despite the kerfuffle, my task came to a safe close. I was free to return to the land of blue, but since I was already here with the living, I wanted to see the award ceremony. However, now that I'd completed my task, any extra contact with the client had the potential to warp the earth. So I decided to sneak over to Yuzu's apartment, careful enough that she wouldn't detect me. She'd already changed into a flowy dress. She looked beautiful in it—as glossy as a black cat's coat. It made me wonder how my fellow trainee Natsuki was doing.

As Yuzu left her apartment, she brought a bundle of trash to the recycle bin outside. On top of the trash sat the yellowed A4 envelope I'd spotted earlier in her room. A breeze fluttered the paper contents around. As I passed by them, I was surprised to see a reservation form for a wedding venue, dated ten years ago. Something must've happened for her to have canceled a wedding.

I recalled what her father had told me.

"As a little girl, she'd always had a hard time dealing with change. No matter her talents or how hard she tried, it never turned out well. She would inevitably fail, or some other kid would beat her to the punch. She experienced a lot of hardship in adulthood, too." But then he'd continued. "But she's got herself to a place where she'll receive an award and host an exhibition. That's good to hear. I'm relieved."

He'd nodded repeatedly, a happy expression on his face.

Now, Yuzu headed for the street and flagged down a taxi. Once inside, but with the door still open, I overheard her tell the driver her destination.

But how would I reach the hotel venue from here? As I pondered the best method, I noticed that the passenger-side door had popped open automatically. It must've been one of those auto-open taxi doors. I quickly slipped inside and snuck myself under the passenger seat.

Once we arrived at the destination, I used the time it took for Yuzu to pay the driver to sneak out. The fact that the driver *and* Yuzu didn't detect me at all just went to show how agile I was.

Yuzu confidently took to the dais. My heart filled with pride. Even her posture had straightened, no hunchback in sight.

"I'm the grand-prize winner, Yuzu Minami," she said into the microphone, looking radiant under the venue lighting. "I'm beyond thrilled to receive such high praise for the art I've spent so much time on. I plan to devote myself even further to improving my craft."

Applause rang out. Among the crowd, I spotted Isobe's face.

"Who would you like to thank first?" the master of ceremonies, who stood on the dais with her, asked. He turned the microphone back to her.

"My father," Yuzu said softly, "who always accompanied me when I went outside to sketch . . ." But then she shook her head softly. "Actually, I think I already conveyed the message, so I don't need to anymore."

She smiled her widest yet.

10

"You finished your first task with flying colors, wouldn't you say?" Nijiko said, cleaning up the café while I gave my report. Café Pont had closed for the day.

I still wasn't happy with my mistake, but I'd eventually gotten it done. "I think I might be cut out for this job."

"There's that smugness again. Now hold out your paw."

I was about to retort when she scratched the back of my neck. She then took my paw and pressed the sole onto my task chart. Seeing that one pawprint stamp made me relax my whiskers.

Just then, a sweet phantom scent crept in from somewhere. I sniffed it for a little while, until I finally recognized the smell.

It was the scent of lotus flowers.

TASK TWO

MESSENGER CAT SEES A CHOCOLATE CAKE

1

"So, Fuuta. How is your job?" Natsuki asked.

I snapped into focus, remembering the black cat lounging next to me under the sun. Natsuki was clumsily grooming the fur on her back.

"My job?" I echoed. "I thought I'd get fired, but it ended up going surprisingly well."

"That's great! Everyone admires messenger cats. My witch cat upperclassmen told me so."

I'd arrived in the afterlife three days before her, so it was only natural for me to take her under my tail. At the same time, I wished she wouldn't look at me so wide-eyed, full of respect. It made me shy. My job title *was* messenger cat, but still.

"What about you?" I asked. "Is work going smoothly?"

By now, Natsuki had stopped grooming and curled into a ball. She lifted her head slightly from its place near her belly and glanced at me.

"I don't know. It's pretty hard. Just balancing on a broomstick is an uphill battle."

She buried her face against her fluffy belly again.

Natsuki had taken a job as a witch's familiar, where she'd been made to mount a broomstick and fly through the sky. She had to cozy up to her witch cat upperclassmen to learn from the ground up. Literally.

"Slow and steady wins the race, right? If it was that easy to fly, the sky would be full of cats," I said reassuringly.

"I don't know if I'll ever fly," came her muffled reply. Seconds later, she softly began snoring.

I watched her back rise and fall. If she was brave enough to sleep in random places like this, I was sure she'd be fine.

Careful not to wake her, I quietly left, and made my way to Pont, tail high in the air.

From the main road, I took the second side street, then a narrow alleyway that led to the café. It was a tight squeeze, just wide enough for one cat. But once I slipped through, the space opened into a nice view of the clearing. The white house in the corner of the clearing was Café Pont.

Now that I'd eaten lunch, completed my daily patrol routine, and relaxed with Natsuki, it was probably around four in the afternoon. Another cat paced by the entrance. It was a black-and-white bicolor cat.

I went to enter the café.

"It's still business hours," he chided me.

Oh right. We weren't allowed to enter during business hours or we'd startle the customers.

"I don't think we've met," the bicolor cat said, rounding his back.

At times like this, it was better not to resist. I didn't want him to think I was challenging his territory.

"I only came to this world about twenty days ago," I explained.

"Are you Fuuta by chance?" he asked.

The sudden name-drop made me inadvertently jump. "Yeah, I am," I replied, a little hesitant.

He slunk toward me, too familiar for my taste. "I heard about you from Nijiko. She said your first job went pretty well."

Ooh, now that was nice to hear. I made a smug sound through my nose. "I guess it did."

"I'm Sky. Nice to meet you."

The fancy English name didn't quite suit his potbelly.

Sky told me he'd been here for about half a year. "Unlike you, my first job went terribly," he said, tears pooling from the memory.

Honestly, I'd initially thought I'd gotten entangled with an obnoxious cat, but his experience could provide useful information for my job.

"Tell me what happened," I pressed, lending him an ear.

"The client had been a woman who was about to get married. She wanted to see her late grandmother."

"Then you should've been able to find the grandmother's address in the land of blue thanks to her nickname, right?"

That was what I'd done for Yuzu. What had him so tangled in yarn?

"That's what should've happened, but my investigation into the client's side of things took too long."

Based on his explanation, the granddaughter had been in a long-distance romantic relationship, which made it harder to pin down her location. As the investigation proceeded, he'd learned that she wanted her grandmother to be present for the wedding.

"You would have just had to entrust the grandmother's soul to someone who'd be present for the wedding, right?" I asked.

"Yeah. That was the plan."

But the investigation had taken too long. By the time Sky

had located the granddaughter and heard the grandmother's side of the story, the wedding had passed.

"So what did you do?" I asked.

"I had no choice but to deliver it after the wedding, during the client's vacation . . ."

"On the honeymoon?"

"Yeah. I made it in time for that. They went to an island down south, where they stayed at a travel lodge. I tried to give the soul to the manager lady who ran the place."

"I see. I bet that made for a fun trip."

"You'd think so." His tears built up even further.

"That didn't go well, either?"

"I went to touch the manager with my tail, but she had a cat allergy. The second I approached her, she started sneezing, and I couldn't get close enough. I ended up giving up on her and entrusting it to the client's diving instructor instead."

He'd learned that the newlyweds had scheduled a scuba-diving excursion, so he'd waited for them on the boat. Just after he'd touched the instructor with his tail, the man dove into the ocean.

"Into the ocean? So he gave the message *there*?" I blurted. I would've panicked, too.

"Yeah. Her grandmother's message was, 'Congratulations. I know you'll be happy.' But I doubt the client would've believed it came from her."

Anyone would conclude that the instructor was giving obligatory well wishes.

"That's unfortunate," I said sympathetically, and I meant it. My task had almost gone sideways, too. I remembered all too well how dejected and powerless I'd felt when I accidentally brushed that little boy with my tail.

"But . . ." Sky's eyes sparkled. "I did manage to get a fish while I was there. A clown fish, I think."

"Ooh, that's a pretty tropical fish. It has orange and white stripes."

"Yeah, that one. But I threw it back into the water right before she resurfaced. This part of the story is just a coincidence, but when the client was a kid, she'd seen them with her grandmother at an aquarium. She'd also watched an animated DVD about one of them at her grandmother's house. When she saw the fish, she seemed to suddenly remember that."

"Then she realized what it meant?"

Sky firmly nodded. "When she surfaced from the ocean, I saw her eyes full of tears behind her goggles. She looked happy, but not from the dive."

"That's great." I exhaled in relief for him.

"And that's how I made it all this way."

Apparently he was now investigating his fourth task as a messenger cat.

"You're almost at your fifth task. That must be nice," I said, envious of him for being so close to the goal.

"It won't be that easy." He frowned. "At first, Nijiko gives us simple targets to arrange meetings for, but the tasks gradually get more difficult."

"Seriously?"

My first task had gone okay, so I'd figured I just had to keep up my pace. This was a big shock.

Sky continued. "This time, I'm helping the client meet someone in the land of green, but I've hit a snag. I'm dropping by here in hopes that Nijiko will give me some advice."

"Both parties are from the land of green?"

"Yeah. I wish they'd just go see each other. But they seem to have special reasons as to why they can't, and digging into that has caused me problems," he replied, shaking his head.

Nijiko only approved requests from customers who had no other options. Surely these people had deep reasons for being unable to meet directly.

"Sounds tough," I said.

My confidence in my ability to complete all five tasks plummeted at seeing Sky so troubled. As he fretted some more, I learned that in his case, he might not even finish all his tasks before the seven-month mark—the end of the temporary ban on passage into the other world—arrived.

"No matter how long I wait out here, the last customer

won't leave. Café Pont won't close. I guess I'll have to give up today and go home," Sky said.

After a quick flick of his tail goodbye, he turned for the road to the land of blue.

Right then, in an ironic twist, the café's door popped open. A woman exited—not Nijiko, but a stranger I'd never seen before. It was the customer Sky had mentioned, who'd overstayed. She was petite and thin, and wore beige cotton pants and a dark brown jacket. Her hair was short and she didn't wear much makeup, which made her look somewhat boyish. She appeared to be in her early thirties. Her feet carried her in a hurry, down the hillside road toward the land of green.

While I watched the woman walk away, Nijiko's voice called from inside the café.

"Fuuta, I know you're there. Come inside."

"You noticed I was here? That's amazing," I remarked, swiftly turning back around and strolling into the café.

Nijiko spread the contents of the letterbox across the countertop. "Wasn't Sky with you?" she asked.

"He wanted some advice, but he got tired of waiting and left."

"I feel bad about that."

I was surprised she paid so much attention to what was happening outside while she worked. How closely did managers have to oversee their employees? I admired—and slightly feared—her for this.

"Want to give this one a try?" she asked, offering me a card. It read: *I want to meet the child.*

"'The child'?" I echoed, shocked. "No other information?"

"The woman who just left wrote it. You ran into her, didn't you?"

I recalled the petite lady with short hair. "I did."

"You must've overheard the story. She told me right here."

"No. I didn't hear a word."

I was too invested in Sky's story to have any idea what was happening inside.

"What were you doing out front? You need to keep your ears peeled," she lectured, then muttered, "Sheesh. These cats."

Nijiko then summarized her encounter with the woman.

"She came to the café just after three P.M. She appeared to be on her way home from work. She ordered hot milk," Nijiko explained.

"Milk? Grown-ups drink milk, too?" I asked.

When I was a kitten, Michiru's Mama would give me milk in a small dish. As I'd lap it up, she'd pet my head and call me a "good boy."

"My hot milk has honey in it. It makes for a subtly sweet drink," Nijiko said proudly.

In my opinion, it didn't seem right to charge money just to warm up some milk. That lady had still ordered it, though, so who was I to say.

"Then what happened?" I asked.

Nijiko reined in her ego over the hot milk and returned to the matter at hand.

"Let's see. After the customer finished her milk, she sat in a daze, staring at the calendar on the wall. Then she started fidgeting."

"Hmph. Maybe she remembered some urgent business."

"It seemed so. When she paid, she asked me for a bakery recommendation. She said she wanted to order an entire cake."

"Sounds like someone is having a birthday."

My power of imagination had grown. Nijiko was always saying: *Improve your imagination.*

"She said her daughter's birthday is coming up," Nijiko confirmed. "So I gave her the name of my favorite bakery. Their cake decorations are adorable. Their top-selling cake is cream puff cake. It's so popular, people line up around the corner for it."

"Cream puff!"

I leaped up on the counter, which had to be three times my own height. Cream puff filling was my favorite food in the world.

Michiru's family had always gotten a cake when one of them had a birthday. Papa would get cheesecake. Mama would get a shortcake adorned with strawberries. As for Michiru, cream puff cake was a given. She'd give me the top part and let me lick the cream off the bottom. It was sweet and melty and fluffy . . .

"Fuuta, are you listening?" Nijiko asked.

"I hear you. You told the customer about a bakery that sells yummy cream puff cakes."

"That's not exactly the point of what I said, but fine. Anyway, the customer's name is Hizuru Soshigaya."

I turned the big card over and cross-checked the customer's name.

"Hizuru took her phone out of her purse and immediately looked up the bakery's website," Nijiko went on.

"She wanted to know where that place was located."

"That's a given. Why do you think she felt the need to look it up immediately?"

"Beats me." I tilted my head. Nijiko had told me to think things through carefully, so I wracked my brain. "A website would tell her the location and business hours. Maybe offer a menu, too? She probably wants to see if they sell cakes that her daughter likes. Something like that?"

"It's more important than that. Think about it: It's her daughter's *birthday* cake. If she wants to order an entire cake, then she probably wants to get one with a message written on it."

My whiskers twitched just before I came to the realization.

"She wants to see if she can get it made in time," I answered.

"Exactly. Every year, Hizuru buys a whole cake with a message plate on top. But this year she's been so busy with work that she's cutting it close. So she panicked and asked me."

"Will she make it in time?"

"The website said she could order as late as three days prior, which she said works perfectly. Then she sighed in relief and left."

"Good for her."

"While she was here, she filled out the *Who do you wish to meet?* survey."

"'I want to meet the child,'" I repeated. "Well, it has to be a child. Maybe one of her daughter's friends?"

"I don't know about that part, but she seemed kind of sad. The next steps depend on a messenger cat. I'm counting on you."

And so, with that, I began my second task.

2

Three days later, when Hizuru would likely return to the bakery to pick up the cake, I made my gallant stroll to the bridge at the bottom of the steep hill, where the land of green and the land of blue connected. At the end of the bridge stood a booth that looked similar to a public telephone. It was one of those police-box things. A husky voice called out to me from inside of it.

"Hey, newbie. How's the job going?"

A familiar tortoiseshell cat—the guard on duty—stuck his head outside. I'd just finished my first task, so he had no reason to call me a newbie. As frustrating as it was, though, I *was* still a baby bird compared to him.

"It's going," I replied, handing him the travel permit Nijiko wrote up for me. It had a cat illustration with a rainbow stamped over it.

"Amboise? Their cakes are delicious."

"So I hear. Don't they have lines out the door?"

"You can't buy the cream puff cakes on a whim. I've never even seen one before. But I know the other cakes pretty well. The fruit tarts are loaded, too. I can't get enough of them," he said, then licked around his mouth.

Apparently I wasn't the only sweets-loving cat. I could've talked about them all day, but I couldn't lose the opportunity to spot my client. I needed to forge ahead.

The tortoiseshell gatekeeper accepted my travel permit and lowered the drawbridge. When it hit the ground, the bakery Amboise was suddenly right in front of me.

"What kind of setup is this?" I wondered.

Every day, this transportation system surprised me. All I could say was that it came with the job.

About ten people stood in line for the bakery. All of them were calm and unbothered, occupied by their phones, spacing out, or reading a book.

Times like these reminded me that humans were so strange. They wasted their time away to hold all sorts of items in their hands. If it were me, I'd give up on the bakery and take the opportunity to find food somewhere else, or find a nice sunny place to sunbathe. Didn't that option occur to them?

I watched the line expand and contract until *I* began to space out. Just when I was about to succumb to my drowsiness, a person's rushed footsteps alerted me to an approaching figure.

I looked up. "That's her."

She wore the same jacket and jeans. The bottoms of her sneakers were worn down and battered.

At first, she went to the back of the line, but then she seemed to notice the one she was in was meant for those interested in buying the cream puff cake. She bypassed the first line to enter the bakery instead. I sidled up to the shop at once, where I could hear her conversation clear as day.

"I'm Hizuru Soshigaya. I ordered a whole cake," she declared brightly. Her tone was comforting.

"Thank you for your patience," the clerk replied, presenting her with a box. "Looks like you ordered a chocolate cream cake. Is that correct?"

The clerk opened the box to show her the cake inside—or at least that's what I assumed was happening. From my position outside I could hear only the sound of a lid opening.

"Wow, it's adorable!" Hizuru chimed.

"Please check the message on the plate, too."

There must've been an edible sign made of some kind of sweet atop the cake.

"'Happy birthday, Himi,'" Hizuru read. "Yes. It's correct."

"And here are those six candles you wanted." I heard the clerk slip them inside the packaging.

After a short while, Hizuru emerged from the bakery with a white box. She cradled it into her chest like it was precious to her. As she began to walk home, I followed, right on her tail—so to speak.

Hizuru's house was located on the corner of a quiet residential area. A simple sign displayed her surname—Soshigaya—on a seemingly newly built property gate. She opened it, then reached the door, where she slipped her key into the lock.

I leaped up on the gate and took my position in the corner of the garden. In a place like this, I could stay a while without giving myself back pain.

I tried to press myself against the wall, but still could hardly hear anything from inside. I heard some things—like when Hizuru changed her clothes and retrieved a drink from the refrigerator—but not much else. Her daughter and husband didn't seem to be home yet.

The garden had several kinds of trees and plants, enough to get one sick on the smell of greenery. I tried licking a petal on one of the flowers, but sadly it wasn't one that I liked. The fluffy heads of a spiky plant swayed in the wind and also caught my interest, but I didn't play with it for long before I got tired of it.

"Everyone's coming home pretty late for a birthday," I remarked.

Stars began to sparkle, and the moon rose into place. It had to be well into night by the time a car finally pulled up to the front of the house and entered the garage. A tall man emerged on lanky legs.

"Welcome home," came Hizuru's voice. It sounded flat. She must've been sick of waiting.

"Sorry I'm late. On her birthday today of all days," he said, sounding genuinely apologetic.

"You remembered."

"Of course I did."

Hizuru remained silent for a beat.

"You bought a cake, right?" her husband said. "Let's eat it."

"Yes. Let's do that," she replied, the brightness somewhat returning to her voice. "I went to a café where I received a bakery recommendation. I decided to order the cake from there this year. I wondered if it was too soon to introduce Himi to chocolate, but I figured a six-year-old's senses would be mature enough to enjoy the taste."

"Right," the man replied shortly.

"Now for the six candles . . ."

Through the window, I could see the flames flickering.

Hizuru and her husband blew them out together, and the light vanished.

"If she was alive, she'd be entering elementary school this year," Hizuru said, her voice thick.

I couldn't hear much conversation after that. Just the clack and scrape of forks on plates.

3

"Hey, how do you think it feels to lose a child?" I asked Natsuki.

She stared at her open book with a complicated expression. It looked like a handbook for witch cats. She'd been stuck on the same page for a while. She eventually gave up and plopped herself on top of it. As she should.

"I haven't had kittens of my own, so I don't know," Natsuki replied. "But some of my friends were mother cats."

Like me, Natsuki had been a domestic cat. But her occasional walks and outdoor gatherings with other cats had given her several feral acquaintances. I had my buddies, too, but we would get into wrestling matches pretty quickly. I didn't remember having any private conversations.

"Giving birth outside made it hard to raise their little ones," she continued. "So they'd take their kittens and search for houses where the humans looked like they might take them in. If the humans didn't seem like they'd accept every sibling, the mother cats would search for a different house for the others."

"That sounds tough."

I didn't remember my cat parents. According to Papa, he'd found me cowering in a bicycle parking lot on his way home from work. He thought I'd been born just a few days prior. He'd initially moved me to a spot where my cat mother could find me, if she'd still been in the area, but ended up taking me home.

"My friends said it was lonely to be apart from their kittens, of course, but their most important hope was that they would grow up somewhere safe and happy."

I'd lived such a happy life at Michiru's house. I bowed my head in silent thanks to my cat parents, whoever they were.

"Some of the kittens lost their lives, though. But that's just . . . nature? Is that the word? They said something like that."

I recalled the silence in the Soshigaya household. Despite the husband and wife's presence, it had been so quiet, as if they weren't there at all.

"It's a miracle to live a full lifespan," Natsuki said with a smile and a twinkle in her eyes.

I was impressed to see how her time with a witch had changed her so much. It gave me a new boost of motivation to fulfill my role as a messenger cat.

4

On the second day of my investigation, I began at Hizuru's house.

I rubbed the sleep from my eyes as I stood on standby beside the Soshigayas' garage. I hated early mornings. Hizuru emerged from the front gate before the sun had fully risen, once again in casual clothing. It seemed her husband was still asleep.

I followed her until we arrived at the entrance of a building. The sign read, KIRINZUKA PRESCHOOL. The building was a single story with a big playground and lots of equipment out front. Despite the early hour, lots of kids were playing.

"Good morning, Mrs. Hizuru," a little girl cheerfully greeted. She carried a pink bucket full of sand. It seemed Hizuru was a preschool teacher.

Hizuru smiled and waved. "Good morning, Mio."

Clearly Hizuru was a caring instructor. I could already tell how much the kids and staff valued her. They'd all brightened immediately, laughter echoing through the grounds.

I tried to sneak into the playground and hide underneath a bench, but a kid spotted me.

"Kitty!"

I ended up getting chased around, and got sick of that *real* quick.

Why did kids shriek at me with such high-pitched voices and no consideration for my well-being? It was unbearable.

As I spent my morning evading distress, eventually afternoon came.

Around this time, the guardians started coming to pick up the kids. The early ones got picked up right after lunch. The same went for Mio, who'd been here since the early morning, playing in the sandbox.

"Mama!" Mio called, running to a woman in a navy pantsuit.

Hizuru, who'd come outside to the playground upon hearing Mio's voice, greeted the mother. "Good afternoon."

The mother nodded at her. "Hi, Mrs. Hizuru. Thank you, as always."

"Mio's become quite the big sister. She's been looking after the other children here, too."

"Wow, really? Well, she'll be starting elementary school

next year. I hope it goes smoothly." She glanced down at Mio's expression.

"Elementary school next year? My daughter also . . ." Hizuru sealed her lips.

"I'm sorry," Mio's mother replied hastily, bowing her head. It seemed she knew what had happened.

"Don't worry about it. It's been very healing for me to work a job where I can perform childcare alongside parents."

"I see."

Mio happily hugged her mother's leg. "We're gonna go look at backpacks tomorrow!" she whispered to Hizuru, peering from behind as if she were revealing a secret.

Hizuru cupped her mouth with her right hand and replied in the same conspiratorial tone. "Are you really? How exciting."

Mio's mother was listening intently. "I hear there are lots of designs on sale these days, and so many colors, you can't possibly choose."

"Back in our day, they designated black for boys and red for girls. We were lucky to see pink," Hizuru added.

"I want emerald green!" Mio said. Before I knew it, she'd pulled a backpack catalog from her mother's handbag and opened it.

"Let me see," Hizuru said, peering at the catalog.

"You can keep it." Mio offered it.

"Mio, stop that," her mother chastised, halting her daughter's hand. But Hizuru had already taken the catalog.

"Wow, there really are a lot," Hizuru marveled.

"If it's not a burden, you *are* welcome to take it." The mother smiled. "I get them from all kinds of manufacturers, and they only end up in the trash."

For a moment, Hizuru's eyes looked pained, but then she returned the smile and waved them goodbye.

Hizuru opened the backpack catalog in front of her husband. It was midnight. He'd only just returned from work.

"Hey, did you know about this? I heard there are several colors available, and there really are," she said. "I wonder what color would suit Himi best? I like lavender, but I think she'd want something cuter. This pale pink one looks nice." Her excited tone continued as she flipped through the pages. "What do you think?"

I heard the hard *thunk* of her husband setting his glass on his desk. I couldn't tell if it was water. It might've been the alcoholic drink he'd had with dinner.

"Just stop it already," he said, low voice echoing. He didn't shout or say it forcefully; it sounded more like a desperate outburst.

"It doesn't hurt anything to imagine it," Hizuru whispered.

"It's been six years. Naming a child that was never born, celebrating her birthday every year, and now planning her transition to elementary school? How long are you going to play parent?"

"So I'm not allowed to daydream? A woman who couldn't birth a child isn't allowed to dream about one anymore? That's not fair. Another woman who gave birth in the same year I did is going to take her daughter to buy her backpack tomorrow. I should be able to imagine that, at least."

"I'm not saying I'm not sad, too. But sometimes I feel like I can't follow you. I'm afraid you can't see the line between daydream and reality."

"I know the line. I take care of other people's children *every day* at work. Sometimes I ask myself why I'm doing that when I couldn't even have a child of my own. But that's my *reality*. I know what it looks like."

Hizuru repeated, *I know, I know*, twice more, then stopped talking entirely.

The same silence as last time then fell over the Soshigaya household.

5

The hearth of Café Pont crackled. Here, it stayed warm year-round—granted, for my purposes, only once evening fell. That was when the messenger cats entered the café. It was probably set up that way in anticipation of our behavior.

I gratefully curled up in front of the hearth, only to smother a big yawn. I was still on the job.

"Babies that die in the womb don't get recorded in the registry in the land of blue," Nijiko said.

"So how am I supposed to find her?" I asked.

During my first task, I'd had to escort the soul of a father. I'd used his alias in the land of blue to track down his dwelling.

"And if she wasn't even born," I pressed, "is she even capable of a conversation?"

My previous client's father hadn't adopted the appearance of his age of death. He existed in this land as he'd appeared in his forties—in the prime of his life. It was what he'd chosen for himself.

"She's growing up in the land of blue," Nijiko replied.

"Is that how it works?"

I supposed a child deprived of life was something that only happened in the land of green. All it meant was that she'd moved to the land of blue. The caveat was that as free as she was, she wasn't registered in the list of code names, so she didn't belong to a fixed place.

"Children that come to the land of blue before or shortly after birth live in a special place within the land of blue. It's something like a preschool," Nijiko explained.

She elaborated: From there, kids then graduated to elementary school, and so on. The boundary between the land of green and land of blue no longer struck me as all that clear.

Hizuru's husband mentioned the need for a boundary between daydream and reality, but that didn't seem necessary, after all. It wasn't my job to tell him that, though. All I had to do was get him to realize it on his own.

"So if I go to that location, I'll find her?" I asked.

"You know her age and name, don't you?"

"Yes. Her name is Himi. She just had her sixth birthday."

"Her name draws the 'Hi' from Hizuru and the 'mi' from Minoru."

"Huh? The husband's name is Minoru? How do you know that?"

"Oh. Did I not show you?" Nijiko offered me the *Who do you wish to meet?* form that Hizuru had filled out. Hizuru *and* Minoru Soshigaya's names were written on the front of the *I want to meet the child* message.

"Huh? So this means . . ." I trailed off.

Obviously the request belonged to Hizuru. But if *two* names were listed on this request, then I had to deliver Himi's words to both of them. I bore double the responsibility.

"If it's too hard, you can just deliver to one of them. The message will have been conveyed either way," Nijiko said reassuringly.

Her words offered me some peace of mind, but was it really enough? Something nagged at my instincts, telling me it wasn't. We orange tabbies had big personalities—and a strong sense of responsibility—after all.

6

The land of blue's preschool was surprisingly easy to pinpoint.

Here, children's residences were arranged to their preferences, and scattered around as much as those preferences dictated. But I knew that the preschool had to be located somewhere the young children could easily commute to. It had to be somewhere central and reachable from multiple locations. Somewhere with a vast playground abundant with nature. That was a must.

"It's probably not on a hillside road," I'd theorized.

The land of blue had a *lot* of hillside roads. Hilltops had nice views and were popular spots for residences, but it would've been tough for kids to go up and down every day. With that in mind, I'd narrowed down the possible locations for the building, and once I found a flat place, I kept going until I encountered the preschool. The imagination I'd been cultivating had paid off.

As soon as I entered the preschool, I instantly found myself surrounded by kids.

"Cute! A kitty!"

I looked for a good escape route, only for a pair of hands to stop me.

"Don't leave! Let me touch you!"

Sheesh. Kids were the same in both lands. I couldn't deal with them.

"Oh? Are you a messenger cat?" a teacher asked, smiling at me as she approached. She scratched under my chin. I wished she'd dial back the games and lesson plans and teach these kids how to handle a cat like *this*.

"Yes," I replied through purrs. "I have a request for Himi Soshigaya."

"Himi? I wonder where she went."

The teacher glanced from side to side, then let loose a giggle. I followed her gaze to a girl who was huddled beneath a desk in the center of the classroom.

"Himi has an excellent eye for art," the teacher explained.

As we approached, I saw she was drawing with colored pencils. The sketch looked like floating soap bubbles. There was a strange warmth to it.

"Is that what you saw in your mother's belly?" the teacher commented. "Himi, you have a guest."

The teacher crouched to Himi's level and introduced us.

"My mommy and daddy want to meet me?" Himi blinked at me with large-pupiled eyes that resembled Hizuru's. "Yay!"

The way she so happily threw her hands up in the air would've made her mother proud.

"If there's anything you want to say to them, tell this kitty cat," the teacher advised.

Himi offered a somewhat troubled expression. "I'm happy that Mommy and Daddy remember me, but I'm doing really good here. I want them to rest knowing that. Besides, I'm gonna be a first grader next year."

Even I was blown away by how cute she looked as she puffed out her reddened cheeks. I supposed kids weren't only loud, obnoxious creatures. I'd never had any kittens of my own, but I got the feeling that I did in fact understand what it was like to have offspring—at least a little.

Parents wanted their children to be happy, and children simply wanted to put their parents' minds at ease. Human or cat, it was all the same.

7

Honestly, I had no plan.

I'd brought Himi's soul with me, but I had no idea *when* I would transfer it for Hizuru. If I did it at her home, I could also share it with Himi's father. But I had a suspicion that that plan could go south.

It was better not to get greedy, so I focused on Hizuru. With my mind made up, I moseyed to her workplace—Kirinzuka Preschool—where I decided to entrust the soul to one of the students.

I waited in front of the school gate at a similar time as my last visit. Hizuru arrived right on schedule. She entered the grounds with a smile and a wave to her students.

"Down to business," I declared.

Step one: I had to choose my target.

Parents were bringing their kids to the school in rapid succession. Just like before, the kids would easily notice and crowd around me—so my plan wouldn't unfold smoothly. Not to mention one wrong move would have me swiping my tail against the wrong person. No way would I emerge from *that* unscathed.

The second the soul transferred, the countdown would commence, since the effect wouldn't last for long. The message *had* to be delivered to the client, or the soul I brought all this way would go to waste.

As for the soul's temporary host, they wouldn't remember anything of the event. In fact, the soul would last for such a brief moment that they'd only feel it physically for a second. They'd have no recognition that they'd ever been used. Nijiko had once explained to me that these messages were only possible thanks to a lag in the space-time continuum between the lands of blue and green. No matter how "connected" the lands seemed, I would have thought it odd if a minor disconnect like this didn't exist between them.

Parents and kids passed me, one after the other, and more time went by as I struggled to commit to a decision.

So long as the soul I'd brought with me stayed in my possession, it wouldn't disappear right away. It'd only be released when I concentrated my energy on making contact with the recipient. Thanks to this function, even if my tail swiped something before that moment, the soul wouldn't escape. Still, like any raw item, it would lose its freshness the longer I held on to it. A withered soul would lose its original "flavor." And a soul's freshness was vital in retaining the sentiments of the soul's owner.

There was one more crucial piece to this puzzle: Cats were forgetful. If we didn't pass along a message quickly, we had a tendency to lose them to the ether. That alone made me impatient to finish this task.

"Panicking won't help me," I reminded myself. "Better to take a second to calm down."

As noon approached, people gradually stopped arriving at the preschool. The kids in the playground reached maximum excitement with no signs of slowing down—and no window for me to approach.

Once afternoon came, I started feeling drowsy.

I'd only meant to shut my eyes and doze off for a second, but when I opened them, I leaped to my feet. The sun was already setting. Even the kids in the sandbox had gone. Only a few stragglers remained inside the school building. If Nijiko found out that I messed up on the job because I'd overslept, who knew how much of a scolding I'd get?

Anyway, I needed to entrust the soul to someone *quickly*. I shook out my back and spotted a girl with a backpack entering the front gate. She was tall and walked with sure-footed steps. She must be older, an elementary-school student.

"Now!" I whispered.

I darted forward and brushed up against the girl's legs, allowing my tail to get a good swipe as she passed. Was it enough? I watched my new host, praying for the message's safe delivery, and followed close behind.

"Hello? I'm Mio Watarai's sister," the girl called out. Her clear voice echoed through the building.

Hizuru poked her head out from a nursery room. "Oh, if it isn't Mio's big sister. How admirable of you to come pick her up," she replied, visibly surprised.

"Yeah. Our dad is waiting for us in the car outside. He couldn't enter the parking lot."

What a good big sister.

But this was no time for praise. The effects of Himi's soul weren't coming out at all. All I could do was watch and worry. It was extremely frustrating.

Mio came running from inside the classroom. "Sis!" she called.

The girl was still baby-like, but in just a few years, she'd have her wits about her, too. How quickly kids grew surprised me. I tried to recall Michiru's elementary school days, but I'd been a kitten at the time, too. It was like a race to see who could grow up faster.

"Ready to go? Mom says she'll return late from work today, but she left something tasty for us to eat at home," Mio's big sister gently told her.

"Really? What did she leave?" Mio asked.

"Cake. She bought some slices before work. She said she got your favorite strawberry cake."

Mio spun around her sister in a chaotic dance of joy.

"And . . ." she went on, but then she looked directly at Hizuru. Hizuru looked bewildered at the sudden eye contact. "She bought *chocolate* cake for me. It's really pretty. It has rose decorations on it," Mio's sister added with a smile.

Mio, still celebrating, didn't seem to hear. She kept spinning and clapping as she chanted, "Strawberry! Strawberry!"

But Hizuru listened to the big sister with her full attention. "You have a taste for chocolate? What about chocolate for a girl as small as Mio?" she asked.

The girl nodded. "It was delicious."

Her voice sounded sweet. Her expression softened—resembling that of a young child's, rather than the face of a big sister or elementary-school student.

Hizuru nodded slowly, as if in understanding. "I see. So you ate it just fine. You're all grown up now."

She watched the girls as they left, holding hands. The big sister wore a light pink backpack—probably the pale pink from the catalog. Hizuru had been right. It would have suited Himi.

Hizuru placed both hands over her heart. "Thank you for growing up healthy," she whispered.

Now that the message had been delivered, I wandered the halls of the preschool for a while longer. Night had fallen. Hizuru had left a while ago. I should've felt fulfilled, but something nagged at me.

A fraction of Himi's soul still lingered inside my body. Even though I'd tried to push it all out, there was something that told me to save a piece.

The request had been for Hizuru *and* her husband, Minoru. And I wanted to deliver a message to both of them. But I'd never heard of such a method of splitting up a soul. And I didn't know how much longer it would last. Maybe one small piece would have no effect at all.

But it didn't hurt to try. I went straight to the Soshigaya residence, where I made it just in time to see Minoru bring his car into the garage.

If he entered the house now, I'd miss my chance. But in a residential area this late at night, it was unlikely that anyone I could use as a host would come strolling by, anyway. Maybe I had to give up . . .

Just as I entertained the thought, Minoru exited his car to

lift the garage door. Something must've been wrong with the electric switch he usually used.

"Here goes nothing," I muttered.

I straightened my tail and darted into place, swiftly swiping it against the body of the navy-blue car. The radio crackled and began tuning.

"Welcome home," Hizuru called. The brightness had returned to her voice.

Minoru sat at the dining table. "Hey, when we have a day off, do you want to go buy Himi a present for entering elementary school?" he blurted.

"What?"

"We still can't buy her a backpack. But what about colored pencils or something? We can have them engraved with her name. That way, we can use them, too. So long as it's something *we* can use and remember her by, I think we should buy it. That kind of thing is okay."

I couldn't hear Hizuru's reply; she'd started crying. Silence then returned to the room, but this time, it was different. It felt as if a soft, bubble-like aura had fallen over them.

"It's so strange," Minoru murmured. "Just now, when I restarted the car to pull it into the garage, the stereo started playing a song from the radio. It was the song I used to sing to Himi when you were pregnant."

"Gosh, you sang that every day. You insisted you could teach it to her in the womb," she said and laughed tearfully.

"Maybe tending to our memories of her is a way for her to grow up," Minoru said gently.

Hizuru nodded. "She's growing up on the other side. I think we can rest assured of that."

8

It had been a *long* day.

Light on my paws, I crossed the bridge and made my way to Café Pont.

"You're rather late," Nijiko remarked from her seat. She'd been waiting inside for me.

"I figured *you* would've gone home already," I retorted.

It was nice to have someone looking out for me, though. I wondered if the fireplace was still going for my sake.

While I gave my report, Nijiko listened, quite engaged. Her eyes widened, she nodded along, and she even cried.

"Well done," she said, wiping away tears. "You granted both of their wishes." She bent over to give me my second pawprint stamp. "It's late today. Go home and get some sleep, okay? Oh, and by the way—I hear that your girlfriend, that black cat Natsuki, will be making her debut as a witch's cat soon."

Natsuki wasn't my *girlfriend*. Sheesh. What a cheeky lady. But how did Nijiko know about that, anyway? There was a lot I wanted to comment on, but I could no longer fight how sleepy I was.

My mouth stretched open in a big yawn. My eyelids were quick to droop. I *supposed* I could take a quick cat nap while Nijiko tidied up the café. After all, the crackling fireplace demanded it.

TASK THREE

MESSENGER CAT PLAYS IN A FIELD

1

Lately, all I could think about was romance. Cats never really had a reason to discuss human love or affection, but strangely, doing so felt like getting caught up in a ball of yarn. Especially after I'd started investigating my third task. I couldn't help but be curious about the topic.

Human love was all about someone you had a connection with, who you got to know, and who you spent time with. The idea that obsessing over each other allowed a couple to live a lifetime of bliss was such a worthless sentiment.

All it took was for one of them to develop suspicions or discover something bad about the other and admonish them for it, or for the other party to start having intrusive thoughts of their own. Didn't they get that making equal concessions and compromises would allow them to meet in the middle?

I turned toward Natsuki to see if she agreed with me, but the black cat was nowhere to be found.

"Natsuki?" I called, looking around me. In the shadow of a tree, only her face was visible as it popped out. A red ribbon was tied around her neck.

"H-how do I look?" she asked nervously.

I remembered seeing a stuffed animal back in the land of green—it had been a cartoon cat with a red ribbon just like that. Tabby cats like me could never pull off that look. It definitely suited her better.

Compared to that stuffed animal, though, Natsuki looked *way* cuter in a red ribbon. Heck, she looked *super* cute. So much so that I realized I was staring, at a loss for words.

"D-does it look strange?" She shyly hid her face.

"It looks amazing on you," I replied.

She pretended to scratch the backs of her ears to hide behind her paws. "Really? I'm flattered," she said. The ribbon around her throat swayed as she spoke.

"But why are you all dressed up?" I asked, suddenly worried. What if she was going out on a date with some random cat?

"This is a witch cat's uniform," she said, fully emerging from her hiding spot to sit in front of me. "I was told to wear this while I'm working."

I recalled what Nijiko told me: Natsuki would make her debut as a witch's cat soon. She'd come to receive encouragement. I'd nearly forgotten.

"You're almost ready," I said. Her training seemed to be going well.

"I'm still full of worries, but I was told that now all I have to do is practice and improve."

"Can you ride a broomstick?" I asked. She'd been grumbling about how hard it was just to mount one the last time I'd seen her.

"I'm not allowed to ride one by myself yet. It's dangerous. For now I've been practicing by riding on a tandem broom behind a witch."

She explained how she'd be given her own broom once she was qualified, but that it was out of reach for now.

"One step at a time, then," I said. For her, and for myself.

My task was a doozy this time around. The investigation itself hadn't gone smoothly at all.

But Natsuki was looking at me with big, round eyes and swished her tail. "Let's both do our best."

Optimistic words from the scaredy-cat she used to be. I answered with a chuff of laughter. "Yeah."

2

Ugh. Every single person was glued to their smartphone.

Whether they were waiting for a train, eating a meal, or walking around, they all kept their eyes on their little screens, as if under a spell.

Yuuji Tougou, the husband of my current client, Fumi Tougou, had been typing away at his smartphone for the last several minutes. Based on the faint smirk on his face, he was texting his mistress, Asuka Nezu.

Messenger cats—well, *all* cats—had excellent hearing, so we could easily eavesdrop on phone calls from a fairly good distance.

But smartphones these days had text messaging and email, and I was sick of it. My eyesight wasn't great. I could read the screen if I was above the phone, but doing so would only draw suspicion during an investigation. Creeping a bit closer didn't close the gap enough to make any of the text legible. At this point, I was ready to throw my paws up.

Based on looks, Yuuji was likely several years older than Fumi, who would turn forty this year. According to Nijiko, his mistress, Asuka, was in her twenties.

"Wipe that grin off your face," I hissed. I continued to tail him, suppressing the instinct to leap out and swipe my claws at the hem of his suit pants. "I feel like a detective investigating an adultery case."

After walking for several blocks, I found myself yawning from boredom, but this was my job. I shook my head and mustered up the motivation to get the job done.

3

I'd taken over this task from another messenger cat.

Apparently, that cat had hit a dead end during the investigation phase, which was when it got handed over to me.

I'd just come off the tail of a successful second task, so I'd had the free time to take it on. Plus, I figured it'd be an easy victory since some of the investigation had already been completed. I was more than happy to pick up the job. But when I immediately smacked into the roadblocks, I realized this wasn't a typical case.

Nijiko had laid out the client's background for me: Fumi had been married to her husband, Yuuji, for ten years. No children. For the last year, he'd been having an affair with Asuka, whom he'd met through work. He had no intentions of breaking up his family, of course. Especially since, on the surface, their marriage seemed to be going well.

"What does 'on the surface' mean?" I'd cut in.

"Humans tend to live their lives in a way that prioritizes outside perception over making waves," she explained.

Made no sense to me. "Not making waves" seemed similar to "making compromises"—the relationship concept I'd been mulling over—but from Nijiko's tone it didn't sound like they were the same thing at all. Not that my job had any room for my opinions.

From what I understood, Fumi had to have been reminiscing about her youth because she seemed to be stuck in a daily cycle where she couldn't change anything.

In her twenties her life had changed course. She'd been a budding singer, still in college, when she sent out her demo tape. As she started to receive audition opportunities, she caught the eye of a small talent agency. Her debut single was chosen as the theme song for a late-night anime series, which gave her a modest start in the industry.

Wataru Honma, her college classmate and the man she'd been dating at the time, encouraged and supported her. However, since Fumi was a rookie singer, romance wasn't exactly banned, but she wasn't allowed to publicly date anyone. As her career progressed, the distance between them grew. She spent more time with her work colleagues than him. Maybe it was destiny that she'd grow close to her current husband, Yuuji Tougou, who'd been an employee at the record company at the time.

Then, all the attention and flattery she'd gotten thanks to her youth passed in the blink of an eye.

After she released her fifth single—before the full album came out—her agency dropped her. As her final reward, her last album was packaged in a way that marked her retirement. It didn't sell well.

Shortly after her retirement, she married Yuuji, who'd been the publicist in charge of that final album. Thinking back, maybe there were some feelings of atonement involved over the fact that the album didn't sell. If so, their marriage had been doomed from the start.

When Fumi had dropped by the café, she'd filled out our *Who do you wish to meet?* survey card and written: *My ex-boyfriend from college.*

The question that haunted her was obvious: "If I'd stayed with Wataru, how would my life have turned out?"

She was searching for the version of herself she hadn't chosen.

4

"Life is a series of choices," Nijiko had said after she'd finished explaining the client's story. "There are some choices that people have to make against their will, but they will still become envious of the paths they didn't choose."

"It's like they say: The grass is always greener on the other side."

I regurgitated the saying as if it were as familiar to me as my own hairball. I'd learned all kinds of strange human customs and figures of speech since I'd started this job.

"That means the grass may *look* greener to *other* people, but it's not necessarily the truth," Nijiko clarified.

"But still," I protested. I was having a hard time wrapping my head around the sentiment. "If a human can't choose both paths, all they can do is keep walking with the belief that they made the right choice."

It was like choosing between crunchy and wet rice. Both tasted fantastic. But if I ate both at once, I'd only feel sick and throw it up later. So, I always went with the one I preferred to eat in the moment. I just had to be honest with myself. Wasn't that enough? How did anyone function if they didn't consider what was valued in the present?

I recalled those irreplaceable moments I'd spent with Michiru. We'd play with a mouse or a stuffed toy on the end of a string. I'd jump down from the top of the refrigerator to startle her, and burrow under her arm to sleep . . . Each of those were moments of happiness, and the reason I felt fulfilled in *this* world.

"Humans spend way too much time worrying about complicated things," I huffed. "The world is a lot simpler."

"True. Regret is a waste of time," Nijiko replied.

But then her expression shifted into something rare enough to make my heart jump: loneliness.

5

"So Fumi's ex-boyfriend, Wataru Honma—is she unable to see him? Did he already go to the land of blue or something?" I asked Nijiko.

Not everyone who filled out Café Pont's survey got to meet their desired loved one. In Nijiko's words: "If the person they want to see is someone they can physically meet, then all they have to do is go."

Which was why *this* client had me scratching my head.

"No." Nijiko shook her head. "He's happy and healthy in the land of green."

So, he was alive.

"Then she can go to him. Isn't that what you always say?" I pointed out. Heck, I had a whole counterargument ready.

There was no need for a second messenger cat to take on *this* particular job.

"I thought the same thing at first," Nijiko relented. "We get a lot of requests to see ex-boyfriends, you see. If we pursued all of them, we wouldn't have any catpower to spare."

Exactly. Still, she cast me a playful wink. I met it with a blank stare.

She then explained the additional details she'd received from the client.

One day, while in a supermarket, Fumi had picked up a bag of potatoes.

"Sometimes the grower's photograph is on the packaging, right?" Nijiko said.

"Oh yeah," I replied. "They use stickers and stuff. They say, 'Picked by me,' or whoever."

I'd seen fresh food like that at Michiru's house, as well as in the kitchens I'd infiltrated during my investigations.

"Exactly," Nijiko continued. "Apparently that photo just happened to be of her ex-boyfriend."

"*Really?* Is he from a farming family?"

Nijiko had no idea about the man's upbringing, but either way, he was currently working in the agricultural industry out in the countryside.

"Then Fumi should be able to use her smartphone to look

up the farm's website," I insisted. Just the word *smartphone* made me want to hiss, but I had to acknowledge how astonishingly convenient it would be for a person to look up and find who they wanted to see.

"The website displays a massive farm, their crops, and photos of the family," Nijiko replied, nodding. Apparently the business didn't just cultivate produce. It was also a sightseeing destination that offered a harvesting experience to touring visitors.

The messenger cat that preceded me had been the one to gather all of this information. To Nijiko, these details explained why Fumi had ordered potatoes au gratin when she visited Café Pont.

"This café makes potatoes au gratin?" I asked. I thought only simple drinks were on the menu.

"Oh, you didn't know? I boil potatoes to a steam, spread them with a white sauce, top them with cheese, then bake them in the oven. They're delicious."

Prideful as she'd looked, I bet that white sauce was from a can off the shelf. Not that it mattered.

I tilted my head. "But if we know all that, there shouldn't be much left to do on this task." I could go to the farm, receive a message from Wataru, then deliver it to the client.

"There's a catch," Nijiko replied, her gaze distant. "Wataru is her ex, and he's living a happy life with his wife and son. How are you supposed to receive a message for an ex-girlfriend from someone who isn't thinking about her? Fumi can't possibly go see him for herself under those circumstances, either."

"Then how about this? Anyone can enter the farm to sightsee, right? She can pretend to be a customer and mix in with the crowd."

Nijiko shot down my brilliant idea. "It's not just about *seeing* him. She wouldn't accomplish anything without a heart-to-heart conversation, now would she?"

"I guess not." I nodded in agreement. It was the same way I wanted to see Michiru; just *seeing* her wasn't enough. I wanted to convey how I *felt*.

"Besides," Nijiko continued, "she'd want him to remember her at the prime of her life. Back when she was thriving and full of dreams."

In the end, Fumi had chosen her career over him. But she'd given up on singing entirely. She couldn't face him now, of all times, when she was knocked down and miserable. At the same time, she had to be wondering what kind of happy future would've been waiting for her if they'd stayed together.

I'd finally understood why the messenger cat before me had had such a hard time with this task. Of course, I was up for the job, but I didn't have the first clue where to start.

6

As predicted, stalking Fumi's husband hadn't offered any new developments. He'd met up with his mistress, Asuka, for an expensive meal at a high-class restaurant, then disappeared with her inside a metropolitan hotel with an ocean view. If I'd learned anything new, it was that Asuka was a budding actress. And Yuuji Tougou was the music producer for her debut movie.

"Always has to put his hands on the closest product," I hissed.

In the cat world, we hated manhandling, too—which was a human habit that seemingly never got better.

7

Unable to watch Yuuji and Asuka together any longer, which only served to put me in a bad mood, I changed the target of my investigation to the client, Fumi herself.

Thankfully, the messenger cat on the case before me had already scoped out Fumi and Yuuji's address. She lived on the twentieth floor of a high-rise apartment complex on a railway line. The neighborhood was filled with luxury apartments. Opposite to the building was a residential construction site piled high with lumber. There'd be big houses on those spacious plots, by the looks of it.

I stood in front of the building and looked up at it. My head practically had to touch my back to do it. "Impressive," I remarked.

Yuuji Tougou must've been making strides in the music industry. I recalled watching him from behind as he practically skipped to his mistress; it left such a bitter taste in my mouth that I wanted to bite him. In fact, it tasted so real that I wiped my face with my paws.

Infiltrating the building wouldn't be too tricky. I could wait behind a potted plant at the entrance, then slip inside after a resident activated the automatic doors. The elevator button wouldn't be a big deal, either—I just had to jump and press the button with my paw. It was best if I proceeded calmly, with no one around to see me do it.

I worried about people potentially joining me in the elevator during the ride up, but the presence of a cat wouldn't necessarily cause any shock. Busybodies could of course always interfere with my plan, thinking I was lost—maybe even go notify building management—but all I'd have to do in that case was run away.

The real problem was what I'd do *after* I reached the apartment.

Most apartment buildings didn't have windows into individual units from the hallways. My only option would be to eavesdrop from outside Fumi's front door. But if she was alone or not conversing with anyone, there was no way for me to collect information. Still, there was always the possibility of TV and video game sounds that could offer some insight into her activities.

I'd had a few other tasks end prematurely after my second one, but at least they'd helped me develop my methodology.

It was time to put it all to the test. I crouched behind a plant and watched for a resident to appear. Then I waited for the right moment to infiltrate the lobby. Inside the building, a man—seemingly management staff—was cleaning the area.

"If I get spotted here, I'll end up in trouble."

I waited for him to leave.

I'd heard from Nijiko what Fumi looked like.

However, her description—forty years old with a large build and a wavy perm—could fit a lot of women, and this apartment building must've housed hundreds of such people. With little information to go on, I struggled to identify her. Quite a few residents had already come and left over the last few hours, but I couldn't figure out which one was her for certain.

Nijiko *had* shown me a photograph of Fumi from her singing days, though. An internet search allowed me to see her CD jacket and listen to her music. Fumi had been unassuming and fair-skinned, with a clear, gentle voice like a fresh spring breeze. My first impression of her voice was that if her music were to be on in the background, it would undoubtedly lull me into a blissful catnap.

Before I knew it, a voice akin to a lullaby caught my ears from somewhere in the distance, ironically jolting me awake. I looked up in a panic, but didn't see the version of Fumi I'd been told to look out for. The owner of the voice was talking to the management staff, but she appeared very different from the picture Nijiko had shown me.

This Fumi had gained double, maybe even triple the weight she'd carried as a singer. Her once-glossy hair showed obvious damage, and her makeup was so thick that I couldn't imagine what she looked like without it. She'd probably spent so much of her youth in makeup, thanks to her career, that her skin had roughened over the years. I was sure she was using makeup to cover *that* up.

But that clear, resonant voice had not changed at all. I was confident in my ears. This was the woman I was looking for.

Fumi's hello to the manager somehow evolved into chit-chat about the weather, before she finally took to the street. I lightly rubbed the grains of sleep from my eyes with my paws, then proceeded to tail her.

After Fumi finished her trip to the supermarket, she stopped at a convenience store. She must have forgotten something.

Both locations were tricky for pets to trespass. I was bound to get chased out if I was discovered inside. So with no other choice, I decided to wait near some hedges. A dog had been left tethered in the parking lot; I evaded its too-friendly advances and paced the glass face of the store instead. It was the perfect place to watch Fumi. She was wrapping up her transaction at the register and getting ready to leave—only to halt. She faced the window, where the magazine racks in the corner of the store waited. She picked one up and opened it.

I managed a glimpse at the cover. Big letters spelled out *Easygoing Country Living*, which must've been the magazine's name. The words *Agriculture for Beginners* indicated it was a special issue, but I highly doubted Fumi's ex-boyfriend, Wataru, would've been featured in there. Yet her eyes were drawn to an article in such a way that I might have believed that she was looking at him. I got the sense she was imagining a different future just to escape from reality, since it wasn't feasible for her to actually run a farm.

Obviously, it wasn't inherently a bad thing to turn away from life's obstacles and sink into daydreams, or find other, new things to enjoy. In fact, I thought that was great. But in Fumi's case, I couldn't help but believe she had better options available than what existed inside her head.

"I just need to obtain the right message to motivate her," I decided.

I headed for Café Pont to receive my next travel permit.

8

At the base of the bridge, inside the police box, the tortoise-shell cat on guard duty was happily grooming himself. He had long fur; he must've been plucking himself to make way for new growth. Strands of fur danced around him in a cloud thick enough to make me sneeze.

"Hey. Working hard, I see." He glanced at the travel permit Nijiko had given me and offered a friendly grin. "Headed to a potato farm today? You're running all over the place."

"That's the job," I replied.

Honestly, I wasn't all that invested in people's happiness. But accomplishing a task made me feel too exhilarated to put into words. Michiru's Papa used to always say, "A beer after work always tastes the best," as he'd reach into the refrigerator and pop a can open. Maybe this was the sensation he'd felt.

Besides, seeing a client happy wasn't a *bad* feeling. I didn't know if it necessarily qualified as *rewarding*, though.

"How many tasks will you have completed once you finish this one?" the tortoiseshell cat asked, though he didn't seem terribly interested.

"Three. *If* I complete it," I answered.

Meanwhile, the tortoiseshell cat began to file the travel permit inside the police box.

I'd made good progress up until the end of my second task, but things had slowed down ever since. I thought back to what Sky had mentioned—that the tasks would get more difficult.

But if I could obtain the right words from Wataru, the message bearer, then this task was bound to go well. I shook out my body and flicked my whiskers, raring to go.

9

A vast expanse of farmland awaited me beyond the downward slope of the bridge. Just as I started stretching my body in the refreshing air, I spotted another cat—a tuxedo cat—inside a human's brown carrier bag. Its emerald-green eyes widened at the sight of me. The cat's human was also pulling along a red travel suitcase. She stopped to flip open a map.

"Are you from around here?" the cat asked me.

"Wait just a second, okay?" the owner told the cat in the carrier, still fussing over the map. She didn't look like she was aware of my presence, even though her cat was literally talking to me.

"No, I'm just here for work," I answered. I debated how much I should say to a cat in the land of green, so I kept it cagey. But his response startled me.

"Are you one of those messenger cats?"

He offered information that suggested he had his own *special* circumstances. He carried the soul of his human's great-grandfather. It wasn't much more than a fleeting conversation between passersby, but I gleaned the gist of his story. He was traveling the country with his human who had plans to open business cafés.

Cats like him had a good lay of the land and a great sense of direction. He'd make a good messenger cat one day, in my opinion. But right now, he seemed plenty busy with his own work; he wouldn't come to the land of blue for a while.

I supposed the land of green had all kinds of supernaturally linked beings, which made me all the more aware of just how unclear the boundary was between the two worlds. It also reminded me of Michiru, and how desperately I wanted to see her soon.

10

A tractor piled high with potatoes rumbled through the field. It must've been harvest season. It seemed visitors weren't allowed during this busy time since I didn't notice anyone who looked like a tourist.

"Should we break for lunch?" A woman's animated voice rang out from across the field. Her appearance startled me. She must've been around Fumi's age, yet she looked so different. She wore denim overalls—if I recalled the term correctly—over a white shirt. Her skin was so suntanned that it looked almost glossy from where I stood. She wasn't wearing much makeup, either.

The boy beside her appeared to be of elementary school age, and he wore pants that matched his mother's.

The boy waved. "Dad, we made your favorite corn croquettes for lunch today!"

"Ooh! Sounds great!" called the man on the tractor. He hopped down with arms spread wide as he approached the two. "The weather's so nice. Why don't we eat outside?"

"Yeah!" the boy agreed.

As I felt their laughter in my ears, I realized this was a losing battle. There was no way I'd pull a message for an ex-girlfriend from this man. I understood why my predecessor had had such a hard time.

Some part of me clung to optimism, though. I'd come so far—there had to be *something* I could find. Maybe he had one of her old CDs, or a token from their relationship. Maybe that was where I could find some words of encouragement for her. But looking at them now, I could tell Wataru's family had no room for an ex-girlfriend from his school days.

"This is hopeless," I mumbled, admitting defeat.

Still, I'd come all the way here. I supposed I could play for a little while, so I wandered the area. I wasn't in the mood to taste test raw potatoes; even the leaves didn't look like they'd appeal to my feline tongue. A little digging in the dirt revealed small bugs, which I batted around for a while, but it wasn't very fun. Cats liked narrow spaces way better than big ones like this, anyway.

Just when I was about to cut my losses and leave, my ears perked up at the father and son's lunch conversation. The mother had left her seat to go make tea for after their meal.

"The tastiest potatoes are gnarly like this, right?" the son asked his father. He looked at the potatoes Wataru had just harvested.

"That's right," Wataru replied. "Come here and look around." They moved to sit in the field, where he elaborated with enthusiasm.

Afterward, his son exclaimed, "So these ones should be ready to harvest soon, too."

"Ooh! Good eye. That's amazing. Really," the father replied, smiling fondly.

I listened to their conversation, a part of me still eager for a message I could deliver to Fumi as the "soul," and thought about how nice it was to have a family.

Even though Michiru and I didn't share blood, she, Papa, and Mama had called me part of *their* family. Now that I thought about it, it had been a strange thing to do. Was that what it meant to have a connection?

The son would probably inherit the farm someday. The potatoes they so carefully raised and harvested would find their way to shelves in supermarkets in the city, then end up in people's hands.

That sure was a wide net of connections. Honestly, I was amazed.

It could've been the refreshing air that had awakened me to this thought, but I was starting to realize that maybe people's limitations were self-imposed. A freer way of life was better, after all.

11

Fumi's high-rise apartment building seemed to stab at the clear blue sky again today. I'd come here yesterday as well as the day before. In fact, I was approaching a whole *week* of visits to this building.

Every day around lunchtime, Fumi only really left the apartment for short walks. She'd go to two supermarkets, then occasionally drop by the drugstore or convenience store. As far as I could tell, Fumi didn't leave home for anything other than shopping.

I hadn't seen Fumi's husband, Yuuji Tougou, during this time, either. Not even once. Maybe he'd been working late, or meeting with his mistress, or maybe he lived somewhere else entirely.

To be fair, as much as I liked to *say* I came by Fumi's apartment every morning, I *did* have my days when I only arrived in the afternoon. And I'd get hungry around nightfall and leave, so my hours weren't exactly set beyond my whims. It was entirely possible that Fumi or her husband commuted during those windows.

The structures in the adjacent construction site had now started to look like houses, so I kept watch over Fumi's apartment building from my hiding spot in a nook of the lumber pile. This spot was a surprisingly relaxing find; I couldn't help but nod off.

But I had to snap out of it or the soul in my tail would lose its freshness. It'd already been ten days since I visited the farm. Even *my* ability to remember everything was starting to weaken.

Not to mention that every day since the start of my investigation, Fumi seemed to be descending deeper into her farm-life fantasy.

During my period of well-intentioned surveillance, I'd spotted a bundle of potatoes in her shopping bag while she was at the grocery store. I only caught glimpses of it, but it was probably from Wataru's farm. As time went on, her shopping bag only got bigger and heavier. One bag of potatoes became two, then the day before yesterday, two became three . . . and just recently, she must've had seven or eight bundles. She'd needed both hands to carry the bags.

That wasn't all. Once every three days or so, she'd receive a delivery. The logo for the delivery company was a cat character. Boy, did those people understand us cats. Whenever I approached them to look at the package labels, they'd carefully watch over me.

I doubted the delivery people were aware of my role as a "messenger cat," but maybe they had some instinctual awareness that we belonged to the same industry. They'd even let me sneak inside the delivery truck and pretend not to see me, for which I was very grateful.

Thanks to one of them, I managed to discover that most of Fumi's deliveries came from Honma Farms. Whenever the deliveryman set the boxes down, he let me see the label on the cardboard. Granted, it was possible that he was merely giving me attention, but I trusted that he was showing goodwill toward me.

So, Honma Farms didn't just sell to supermarkets. They also received orders placed online. Fumi must've found that option on their website and bought a series of items. It looked like she'd been purchasing them in her husband's name, so Wataru likely hadn't realized it was her.

Maybe Fumi figured this was a way of supporting Wataru in secret, but her behavior was reaching abnormal territory.

Her husband wouldn't come home. She had no children. She had no savings to make it on her own. And her kitchen must've been overflowing with enough potatoes to start her own farm.

I gave a short hiss. "This isn't good."

At this rate, Fumi would only torture herself, if she wasn't already. I had to hurry and bring her back to reality with Wataru's words—and soon.

As much as I'd wasted the day away watching for an opportunity to entrust the soul somewhere at this construction site, a good moment never came.

I could've tried entrusting it to another one of the apartment building's residents, but Fumi didn't seem all that acquainted with them. She wouldn't have had a reason to hold a conversation. And the manager didn't like cats. Unlike the delivery people, he wouldn't let me get close enough to swipe my tail. Maybe he was busy.

Earlier, I'd declared, "Today is the day." But it didn't look like I would succeed today, either.

Sunlight cut into my hiding spot inside the pile of wood and warmed my body. The wood shavings that the carpenter had left behind danced around in it. I batted the fine, fibrous materials, and I eventually grew drowsy.

"Good things come to those who wait," I told myself, yawning.

That was how the saying went, but ... this was the perfect nap spot.

Just as I curled up, I heard a large board set against the pile, as if someone was readying it to be cut up. There was a round gap in the center, but it wasn't the kind of hole that looked purposely made. It looked like a big knothole had crudely popped out while the lumber was in the process of being cut.

I looked through the hole. I doubted I was the only cat who'd have the impulse to go through it. If a cat could fit their head into a certain space, their body could squeeze through, too. As long as they weren't too chubby, anyway. *My* trim body had plenty of wiggle room. I stuck my head out and slipped right through. My sleepiness had vanished. I forgot about the time and happily weaved back and forth through the hole in the board.

During my umpteenth turn, I found myself facing the road—just in time to see Fumi exit the building.

"This isn't the time to play," I chastised myself.

I quickly reentered work mode, panicking a little, which made my body catch partway through the hole. I reset my posture, then slipped through without much difficulty, but I'd made one little mistake in my excitement. I'd unknowingly puffed up my tail, the soul collecting there. Worst of all, after I'd made it through the hole, my tail had touched the wood.

Souls didn't only transfer to humans. They could transfer

to objects, too—and I'd just transferred it into a useless cut of wood. It was all over. I couldn't take a soul back. I would have to return to the farm to retrieve it again. All I could do now was watch Fumi cross the street as I blamed myself for playing too hard.

"Hey! Grab the plank that's propped up!" instructed the foreman.

"Got it!" chimed the young male carpenter. He lifted the board I'd just been playing with.

"Uh-oh. That board has Wataru's soul in it . . ." But I couldn't do anything about it. The soul would be carried away.

That was when Fumi started walking by the construction site. A potential outcome crossed my mind—if she could just touch the board, the soul might transfer to her—but all speculation was hopeless.

The foreman examined the board. "What is *this*? It's full of knotholes. Just like *you* are," he chided, then directed the carpenter to bring him a different board.

"Like me?" asked the carpenter. He scratched his head.

"I'm saying you've got knotholes for eyes. You're not observant."

His tone got rougher. I couldn't tell if he was angry or teasing. I strained my ears, hoping something meaningful might come from their conversation. Fumi, who now waited for the crosswalk signal to change, must've been within earshot, because she'd turned to look. Maybe she thought the exchange was funny, or maybe she was gazing at the houses in progress—either way, she was paying attention.

"Boss, don't you think that's harsh? I don't have knotholes for eyes!"

"Yeah? How's that?" The foreman sounded irritated.

"Because I *am* observant. I mean, I see the benefits of working under you. I'm bound to become a fantastic carpenter that way. I respect you a lot."

"If you've got time for flattery, get to work!" the foreman shouted, throwing his hands in the air as if to startle him. Heck, he'd startled *me*.

"I *have* to be observant just to be here." The carpenter grinned as he went to place the board in the pile of materials near the street.

"So what are you saying? Everyone who comes through here ends up becoming accomplished?"

"I don't know if they'll succeed at this, exactly, but I'm positive they'll be happy with their choice to try."

"You got a lot of confidence saying that. I guess that means progress on this site will go smoothly and we'll build some nice houses."

"I don't know the way forward, though," the carpenter replied, his tone suddenly dropping.

My whiskers swayed in the soft breeze. It smelled just like the air at the potato patch.

"Come on, hop to it!" the foreman yelled.

Laughter enveloped the construction site. However, the carpenter turned his face to the street, then whispered clearly. "I know happiness is still within reach. I *am* observant, after all."

After that, the board he'd propped on his shoulder tipped him backward. "Whoa!" He laughed.

The foreman was already picking out a new plank, no longer listening. All that followed was the upbeat echo of tools.

But Fumi's eyes had widened at the carpenter's final exclamation. The signal light turned green, but she stood stock-still, staring as if stunned.

Something Wataru's son had said at the farm surfaced in the back of my mind. They'd been talking about what made a good or bad seedling.

"Dad, do you ever know if a seedling will grow for sure?" he'd asked. His father was obviously his hero.

"I sure do. See, these eyes of mine aren't just for show. I'm *observant* to how people grow. Just look at your mother. I had to have a sharp eye to score the wonderful mother she'd turn into. Whoa! See?" He laughed, spotting his wife emerge from the house with a tea set on a tray. "And the same goes for others I've engaged with meaningfully. I have faith that they're all happy now."

Fumi's face reflected in the window of the building next to the construction site. Her expression looked tired with age. She stroked her cheek with her right hand. Maybe she was pitying herself for her exhaustion, or possibly wiping away tears.

A neighborhood notice had been taped to the window. The poster advertised a piano recital that was scheduled at the nearby community center. Fumi's eyes practically chased the words across the page. Maybe she was envisioning herself back in her prime, organizing a collaborative performance with a pianist from her hometown. She *was* a former professional singer, so she could even teach music as a private tutor, or instruct a class at a public facility.

She would discover a way for her current self to live without shame. She'd move forward by herself, get back on her own two feet. Maybe she'd even choose to leave her husband. That way, she could be proud of her past *and* future. But that wasn't for me to find out. I was sure she'd find her way eventually.

12

Fresh off my debrief, Nijiko declared, "Goodness, you're such a scatterbrain. But this task was hard won for everyone, so let's consider the matter settled."

She gave me my third pawprint stamp.

But there was one detail I'd left out of my report.

On my way back from Fumi's apartment complex, I'd dropped by a certain building—Yuuji Tougou's office. I waited until evening for him to leave work, where he fell into his usual routine of fiddling with his smartphone before meeting up with his mistress, Asuka.

I tailed them to that same metropolitan hotel and, just as they were about to enter, sprayed his expensive-looking trousers. What exactly did I *spray*, you might ask?

My *urine*.

Yuuji had simply looked puzzled at the sudden cold, wet feeling on his pants. It was Asuka who'd reacted quickly.

"Hey. You kind of stink," she'd said, giving him a suspicious stare.

"Huh? I do?"

He probably didn't believe he was the source. Asuka pinched her nose and grimaced. "Ugh. It reeks! I'm not in the mood anymore. I'm going home."

She turned away in a huff and ran off as if trying to escape. Yuuji started to go after her, but stumbled. His damp pants must've twisted around his legs as he'd turned.

I'd watched the scene unfold from a nearby hedge. It was quite the show. Even thinking about it now nearly had my belly in stitches.

13

The messenger cats had all gone home for the day. Silence fell over the inside of Café Pont.

Alone, Nijiko put away the dishes and ruminated over the day's events.

"I hope everyone managed to meet the people they wanted to meet today," she said softly.

The messenger cats in her employ had been fighting hard to get their tasks completed. Even Fuuta—the new recruit—was gradually getting the hang of his job. As the business owner, she was pleased with his growth.

"But how many of these must I do before I'll be forgiven?" she mused.

Would the day ever come when she forgave *herself*?

Soon, the wood in the fireplace would burn down to its final embers.

Nijiko hurried to put everything away.

TASK FOUR

MESSENGER CAT BASKS IN A PLAYGROUND BREEZE

1

Elementary school teacher Tohru Ochiai sat in a folding chair in front of the podium in his fifth-grade classroom. The kids had left for the day, so no one else occupied the classroom. Still, the air of activity lingered.

The knit cardigan he wore over his white shirt was pilling, and the fabric at the elbows had thinned. This was only natural; he'd been wearing the garment ever since he'd started his job here. Soon he'd reach his twentieth year as a teacher. Now that he was over forty years old, his hair had started to turn gray. He ran his hand lightly over it.

2

I stood with Sky outside Café Pont to kill time. It didn't look like any customers were inside, but Nijiko would scowl at us if we entered during business hours. So, I napped and tussled with Sky instead.

Sky had already finished his fifth task and, joyously, met his loved one. His coat looked much glossier than it had when I last saw him. Maybe his loved one lived by the ocean and gave him tasty seafood to eat. The big meow he let out proved just how happy he was.

He said he'd come to Café Pont to give his final greetings to Nijiko, now that he'd completed his role.

"What will you do from now on?" I asked him. "Continue as a messenger cat?"

"I think I'll take it slow for a while and carefully consider my next move."

The easygoing route, then.

That prompted me to ask the question that had been poking at my curiosity: Why was Nijiko tasked with this job, anyway?

Nijiko belonged to the land of green, as we'd coined it.

"Nijiko seems to carry some feelings of repentance toward a pet cat she once had," Sky offered. "Maybe her regret inspired her to hire cats from our world as a way to do a bit of good." He'd heard the story from another messenger cat. "I don't know what happened with hers, but cats are just happy to be cared for. She shouldn't let it bother her."

"Humans sure worry about unnecessary stuff. Instead of fretting, she should focus on enjoying the present," I replied.

Sky swatted at me with his paw. I took on the challenge. Riled up, Sky reared back a bit, took aim, then lunged at me. I pounced on him, just as resolute.

"Grrrr!" I growled.

Our scuffle went down like a professional wrestling match, though it probably looked like a real catfight to others. There were moments when we got too carried away and scratched each other, but our wounds always healed quickly once we licked them. We couldn't help but have fun.

In the peak of afternoon, after we'd had our fair share of

exercise, satisfaction filled me. Sky started snoring away. *I'd better take advantage of this time . . .* I thought, and curled myself into a ball, too. Just then, I saw two men ascend the hill that led toward us.

"This place is called Café Pont. It means 'bridge' in French," one of the men told the other. They must've been looking for a spot to take a breather. "Want to go here?"

This was the first time I'd heard that *pont* meant "bridge." I wanted to tell Sky about it, but he was sound asleep.

The men approached the front door. They gave off the impression of energetic professionals in their late twenties. The one who'd read the sign was somewhat short in stature. He wore cotton pants and a jacket. The other man was also dressed in casual attire, but with denim jeans and a black knit turtleneck. He nodded, entering the café.

I shook off the drowsiness that had crept up on me and sidled over to the window. When I was a newbie and I'd played outside waiting for closing time, I'd usually fail to observe what was happening inside and Nijiko would give me a big scolding. Now, though, I made sure to listen in on the conversations that took place. The fact that I even thought to do this proved I'd grown.

"Welcome," Nijiko said, coming to greet them.

The two men took their seats.

"Do you have beer?" one of them asked.

Uh, no, we don't, I wanted to cut in.

"We do," Nijiko chimed.

I hadn't expected the café to serve alcoholic drinks. While I stood dumbfounded, I heard the sound of beer being poured, then the *clink* of the men tapping their glasses together. Their merry voices followed.

"I couldn't even get drunk back there," the jacket-wearing one complained.

"Seriously. I'm glad we went out for another round. Thanks for the invite," said the man in the turtleneck. He sounded mild-mannered.

"I can't believe Kawase has a kid already."

"That's for sure. Not to mention Mogami's completely transformed."

"He was the tall, skinny scarecrow compared to the rest of us throughout elementary school. Now he's all muscle in a suit."

As I listened, I organized the information in my head: The two men were friends from elementary school, and they'd just left their reunion party. They'd come here to continue drinks and conversation.

"Oh man. I'd been secretly hoping to see Emi again, but alas," the smaller man groaned.

"Emi Hoshina? You had a crush on her forever. You were never going to have a romance bloom at the reunion, though.

Hosokawa—she organized it—told me Emi had to work today."

"Ugh. Too bad. I wanted to see her."

My whiskers twitched at the statement, but it seemed I wasn't the only one who'd caught it. Nijiko did, too.

"Did you just say you wanted to see someone?" she asked, returning to their table.

"Yeah. She's our old classmate from elementary school. We had our reunion today. It's been fifteen years since we graduated," the smaller man explained.

"The reunion must've been fun," Nijiko replied brightly.

Turtleneck sounded exasperated. "Yeah, but he didn't get to see *her*, and so he's brooding."

"Ah. Now I understand."

Nijiko brought over the *Who do you wish to meet?* survey cards and explained how they worked.

"So if I write, 'I want to see my old crush, Emi Hoshina,' then I'll encounter her?" the smaller man asked excitedly.

"It means you *might*. It *is* just a survey form. Your wish to see her won't be granted if all you do is *think* about seeing her," Nijiko clarified.

"Yeah, but I can't just *go* to her, you know?" He looked to his friend for help.

"Wouldn't Hosokawa know her contact information?" Turtleneck asked.

"I guess so, but—"

"Then don't get so flustered about this," Nijiko admonished. "If you want to see her, just go see her."

"Right," the smaller man said with a sigh. He sounded dejected—or maybe he got nervous just imagining the meeting. "But the people we want to see aren't exactly . . ."

He trailed off, eventually writing the name on the survey form. After Nijiko returned to the kitchen, Turtleneck chose to speak.

"I think *I* want to see Mr. Ochiai," he said.

"Our teacher? We just saw him."

"To be honest, I went to the reunion today to teach him a lesson."

"Mr. *Ochiai*?"

"Yeah. I wasn't exactly popular in elementary school, remember? Sure, I hung out with you, but still."

"I suppose Hosokawa's good grades and that pretty girl Onoue hogged the spotlight. Parents wouldn't let favoritism fly these days, but back then, it was easy to tell that certain students were treated better."

"It's not like I was bullied or given corporal punishment, so I don't *really* care at the end of the day. But there's one thing I could never let go."

He described their second semester in sixth grade. Most students were planning to attend public middle schools in their hometown, but several kids from affluent households with education-obsessed parents were being forced to take exams to get into private schools. Onoue, who'd been known for her good looks, was one of them.

"I got the sense that my mediocre grades fit somewhere into the top half of our class, at least, but I was *excellent* at math," Turtleneck said.

"I remember that. You helped me with my homework."

"I usually did it *for* you."

The two of them laughed.

"That's why I didn't care so much about my grades in other subjects," he went on. "I never got less than ninety percent in math."

"That's amazing. That's an A no matter what. My parents never expected much from me. So long as I wasn't failing, I was good."

"*Whoa.* Is your family business doing okay?"

Apparently the smaller man had inherited an automotive sales business. He said they had a lot of wealthy customers, and some foreign ones. They must've sold foreign model cars.

"Anyway, grades from the second semester of sixth grade served as the transcript portion of the exam students' applications. So there was a rumor that teachers tended to give good grades to the exam takers. Remember that?"

"Yeah, I definitely heard a rumor along those lines."

"That was the only time my math score ever slipped a grade. Our tests followed the same pattern as they always had, and I hadn't forgotten any homework assignments, so I was shocked. And when Onoue got *her* report card, she was baffled by her good grade. She'd yelled, 'Wow, I got an A in math!' She even sucked up to Mr. Ochiai with statements like, 'I'm just so *happy*, Mr. Ochiai!' I'll never forget his face when he heard that. He looked *proud*, like he actually cared about a student."

Turtleneck went on, giving the caveat that he obviously didn't know what had actually happened. Maybe his grades that semester weren't as good as he thought. Still, he was frustrated. He wanted to rub his current success in his teacher's face.

"You're so accomplished now. I'm proud of you," said the shorter man.

"Thanks. But now that I actually got to see Mr. Ochiai again, he didn't even remember who I was. There was no way I could give *him* a lecture about his favoritism without his memory of it. Talk about anticlimactic." He smiled bitterly. "I wish I could go back in time with everything I know now and *then* confront him."

"Ooh, that would be nice. I hear he's teaching at Matsushiba Elementary. Is that where your elementary-aged self would give him a verbal smackdown? I bet that'd feel *amazing*." The shorter man laughed loudly and got up to head for the kitchen. "Excuse me, miss?"

He looked tipsy. He didn't sound slurred, though.

"Sorry, but your request isn't possible. We don't have a

time machine here," she replied curtly. She must've overheard their conversation.

"I see. That's too bad," he said, then returned to the table and patted Turtleneck's shoulder, looking vexed.

"A child doesn't have to deal with bullying, irrational parents, abuse from a teacher, or any newsworthy incident for them to feel hurt," Turtleneck said firmly. "Little things can chip away at them, too. Being forgotten or left behind is hard enough to bear. I just wish I could have had even the briefest of moments to make Mr. Ochiai realize this. It might allow him to spare a kid or two those same feelings."

"Yeah," his friend agreed. "Heck, I think *I'll* reflect on how I treat the employees under me. Gotta make sure I'm facing them like equals."

"Oh? You have that many subordinates?"

"'Subordinates' is a loaded word. About half of the staff from my father's time have stuck around, so they're really my *superiors*. But I'd gotten it in my head that they'd treat me like an idiot if I admitted it. Hearing your story has changed my mind."

He raised his fist in a gesture of determination, swearing to act on his newfound feelings starting tomorrow.

"Well, those memories gave me a backbone, so I suppose I have to thank Mr. Ochiai for that," Turtleneck said, then finished off his beer.

3

"So, what do you think?" Nijiko asked me as she took the beer glasses away. The customers had long left.

"The first crush request isn't happening. He can just go see her himself," I replied.

In fact, while he'd been writing her name on the survey card, he'd muttered something to himself: How even if he submitted the survey, it wouldn't accomplish anything. He'd decided to give up on the request and act on his desires for himself. If he was willing to say that, it was better for his sake that I *didn't* choose to arrange a meeting.

"That's not the one I meant," Nijiko replied. She spread out the contents of the letterbox.

"You mean the man who wants to see his teacher? You're the one who said we don't have a time machine."

"Of course we don't. It's impossible to turn back time. But his request is nagging at me."

I shared the sentiment. The teacher they'd mentioned—Mr. Ochiai—seemed like the type of guy who worked for his own self-preservation and gain instead of the kids. He gave me the creepy-crawlies. Naturally, the mere thought of bugs riled me up.

"On that note, I'm leaving it to your imagination to do something about it, Fuuta," Nijiko finished.

"'Something' leaves a lot of room for interpretation . . ." I grumbled.

The client's name—Susumu Hirose—was written on the front of the survey card. She opened it up to show his request.

I want to see Matsushiba Elementary School teacher Mr. Tohru Ochiai and teach him a lesson.

As I approached it, my nose twitched.

"Huh? I still sense his presence here," I realized.

Nijiko looked up. "Then why don't you take the bit of soul that Susumu left in this card to Mr. Ochiai? You heard everything he wanted to say, so that must include the message, right?"

"You're telling me to deliver the *client's* soul to the person they want to see?"

"Exactly. Then you'll entrust it to a third party to convey it. It's the reverse of our usual pattern, but you get the drift."

Was this possible? I ran a simulation in my head.

"But this means Susumu, the client, won't get to encounter Mr. Ochiai himself."

"That's true. For this task, we will be taking the initiative to get justice on Susumu's behalf. He won't know that we did this."

"So the message doesn't have to be *his* words, then?" I checked.

Nijiko nodded, firm.

Susumu was already succeeding in life, and he'd already overcome his old scars; he was doing fine now, in Nijiko's opinion. In a way, this was our own *extracurricular assignment* of sorts.

"Anyway, all you have to do is show Mr. Ochiai who's boss, and maybe make him reflect on himself."

Perhaps relieved to have delegated a new task, she returned to checking the rest of the survey cards. A moment passed before she spoke again.

"Oh my," she whispered. Her hands had stopped on a card. Just after her eyes widened, she let out a snicker.

"What is it? Did you find a funny request?" I asked. "Let me see!"

She hid the card behind her back and grinned. "No can do. I must respect the client's privacy."

"Hiding it only makes me more curious."

Cats were like that. There was nothing more fascinating to us than a piece of paper peeking out from behind a desk, or maybe a balled-up receipt hidden underneath a curtain. I made my complaints, but Nijiko continued to turn me down.

"Fuuta, you need to concentrate on your job. This task isn't requested by the client himself, so just relax. Work is work, though, so if you succeed, I'll give you another paw-print stamp."

That was fine by me.

I got ready to make my way to Matsushiba Elementary School to find Tohru Ochiai.

4

At the head of the bridge, the tortoiseshell cat guard was making a nihilistic expression. He hadn't noticed me approach the gate, so I called out to him. Maybe he was feeling sick or something.

"Hey," I said.

"Oh. Messenger cat."

He snatched my travel permit. He sniffled, at odds with his brash body language.

"What's the matter? Have you been crying?" I asked.

"Shut up."

I shut up.

But I still worried. "Did something happen?"

"We meet people with all kinds of life stories while we're here. You know how it is," he remarked vaguely.

"Well, yeah. That's just how humans are, right? Their species can have all sorts of experiences. It's interesting," I offered.

He clumsily scratched behind his ears with his thick front paws. "So, you're off to an elementary school today? Are you delivering a message to a kid?"

Now that he was back in work mode, the tortoiseshell cat skimmed Nijiko's handwriting on my travel permit.

"No. The client wants to see his old teacher," I replied. "But this task is a bit irregular."

I couldn't tell him any specific details. Sure, he was a guard, but messenger cats had to abide by confidentiality.

"If you succeed, how many tasks will you have completed?" he asked, his tone lighter now.

"Four."

"That many already? You're closing in on the goal." He said it like a coach to their player.

Our conversations rarely carried this kind of flow, so I figured I'd take the opportunity to ask a question of my own. "Don't *you* have anyone you want to see?"

"I was a loner cat. Unlike the spoiled ones such as yourself, I was born and raised in the wild. I did a lot of bad stuff to survive."

I doubted my imagination could tell me exactly how hard it was to live as a stray, constantly enduring the rain and cold with no end in sight. I kept quiet.

"But don't feel sorry for me. I got to live a free life," he added with a sharp glance which, admittedly, made me flinch a little. He continued, as if recalling his memories. "I stayed in one hideout for a short time, though. That house had brats that shrieked like nothing else."

I understood his intolerance for children's voices all too well.

"But someone fed me every night. So I kind of stuck around."

"I've heard of 'community cats,' where people in the general area take care of them. Was it like that?" I asked. I'd met cats like that around Michiru's neighborhood.

"I'm not sure. I couldn't tell who actually gave me the food. I'd just eat what was put out for me."

He went on to explain how that had ended one fateful day, when he went to get his usual food. There'd been nothing there.

"Were you able to endure the hunger?" I asked.

"I was a wild cat, you know. But there I was, totally trained into going to eat my food at the same time every day. I had no patience. I was hungry and I wanted to eat, so I left my hideout and moved someplace else." He spoke plainly. "That kind of thing wasn't unusual."

"Sounds rough," I said before I could catch myself.

"I told you not to feel bad for me. I never liked staying in one place."

I couldn't tell whether or not he was putting on a brave face.

"There *was* something I learned way later, though." Apparently from the cats that patrolled the neighborhood. "I don't know if it was that family or a neighbor, but some *rat* called animal control. They planned to send someone out that very day."

"Meaning . . ."

"Yeah. I would've been taken and euthanized."

The way he came out and just *said* that made my heart race.

"Then I guess it was a good thing that you got out of there so fast," I marveled.

"Sure was. I heard later on that those noisy brats had picked up on the plan and stopped giving me food so I wouldn't come back."

Supposedly the human from animal control had been flustered. The food he'd set out—as a trap—had disappeared. The children told their parents that a crow had flown off with it. For a while, the parents put up netting to keep the crows away.

"I felt bad for the crows," he said. "They did their fair share of bad stuff, too, but they had good moments." He sniffled once, maybe to cover up his embarrassment. "So, all this is to say, sometimes I think I wouldn't mind meeting those kids."

"When the time comes, you can have me deliver the message."

"Yeah. Maybe I will someday. They're all adults now, though."

He looked off into the distance and huffed a laugh.

Onoue had grown up being pampered. Whereas Susumu had climbed his way up to a CEO position with his own abilities. This wasn't a matter of whether either one of them had lived their life the "right" way. That didn't exist. The way I saw it, though, Susumu's life path—in which he'd struggled and cursed and raced to the top—was more beautiful.

Some humans would never know struggle, but others would harbor failure and regret. Perhaps there was no competing with the beauty of someone without scars, but the ones who'd healed their scars emerged from their experiences with greater strength. Had Tohru Ochiai been the kind of teacher who taught that, he probably would've been loved.

This was the realization that had come to me after seeing the tortoiseshell cat, and all the scars he carried.

5

Matsushiba Elementary School had about five hundred students.

I found Mr. Tohru Ochiai's classroom immediately. A floor plan of the school had been posted at the entrance, with each teacher's name written on it. I'd been worried about whether the classroom was on the top floor; if so my only option would've been to jump up on the veranda to peek inside. Luckily, Mr. Ochiai's class—fifth grade, class one—faced the garden on the ground level. I stretched my back and placed my front paws on the windowsill.

At a glance, the classroom had roughly thirty kids inside. Mr. Ochiai stood in front of the blackboard, eyes lowered to a textbook. One of the students raised a hand and stood. He wasn't asking a question. He was turning the pages, reading the contents aloud. It must've been a language class.

The student had read several pages by the time Mr. Ochiai interrupted him.

"Okay. Stop there. Who's next?" he snipped.

The student sat. Another student in the front row enthusiastically raised his hand.

"Would anyone else like to read?" Mr. Ochiai asked with an exasperated expression. "If you must, then. Mitsui." He faced the student in the front row and lifted his chin.

"Yes, sir!" The student shot up from his seat and read the next passage. He read every word with clarity, but it must not have been fast enough for Mr. Ochiai's liking.

"Can't you read smoother?" he sneered. "Enough. Stop there." His command came with a big sigh. "We don't have time. Sakurai, will you read the rest for us?"

His tone had changed. The child he'd pointed to—a student in a center seat—wore her long hair in a ponytail. She stood quietly and read the rest with perfect flow. Mr. Ochiai nodded, looking satisfied. Just then, the bell chimed, signaling the end of the class.

I wracked my brain over whom to entrust the client's—Susumu's—soul to. I thought about choosing one of the children, but now that class ended, they'd leave the classroom and disperse across campus. There wouldn't be a good opportunity for them to talk to a teacher.

I could make them speak up *during* a class, but that wouldn't come across as natural. I aimed to make my selection during their lunch break, but it was hard to target someone in a fixed spot. Maybe because they'd grouped up to eat.

This *Mr. Ochiai* was a tough opponent—but not in the sense that he was strong-willed or unusually powerful in some way. I didn't know whether the expression "hard to stomach" was correct, but what I *did* know was that I wouldn't want to be near someone like him. Obviously I didn't want to eat him, either. I doubted just a few words would be enough to jolt him.

To really "teach him a lesson," I needed help.

Meanwhile, lunch break came to an end.

An art lesson was on the agenda for that afternoon. The highly structured curriculum had taken two hours to get through. At the beginning, Mr. Ochiai declared that the students would submit their watercolor paintings—a topic they'd been studying for nearly two months—today. The book they'd read aloud in language class—a Kenji Miyazawa novel—had provided the theme. The students were free to interpret the world as they imagined it.

These days, cross-curriculum lessons like this—as opposed to independent subjects—were becoming commonplace. It seemed that the board of education was requiring it, so schools had been implementing them.

After the lesson, Mr. Ochiai lifted the haphazard pile of paintings his students had submitted and clacked them against the desk until the papers arranged themselves into a tidy stack. The artwork had been submitted from the back row to the front, so he'd collected them in a predetermined order. The drawing at the top must've belonged to a student in the front row. It depicted a starry sky. The paint looked wobbly on the construction paper, like it hadn't quite dried yet, but he didn't seem to care.

He flipped the stack of artwork face down without hesitation. The students had written their names and seat numbers on the back; he must've instructed them to do that.

He looked at the names, paper by paper, and placed one of them on the right side of the desk, then went on to place a select few more on top of it. The class had just over thirty students, but once he'd finished reading all of their names, only six or seven papers had been stacked on his right. Finally, he turned those over to see the actual artwork. The other twenty-plus paintings didn't receive a single glance. In fact, he ungraciously stuffed them inside an envelope he'd prepared.

He hadn't chosen those paintings for their art. He'd selected them based on names. Whether the remaining seven or so students were just *that* good at art, had the best grades, or were simply Mr. Ochiai's favorite students, was unclear. The fact of the matter was that they were his chosen few.

It wasn't those children's fault. He'd simply taken a liking to them. The ones who stood out for their excellence were the ones who demonstrated effort and talent, after all. But how did the forgotten ones feel? If they managed to produce a good painting today—to effectively express the world of the novel as they'd interpreted it—did Mr. Ochiai dismiss their work as a coincidental, rare success that didn't deserve evaluation?

How awful.

Anger rippled through me, but just then the classroom door rattled open.

6

As the door opened, Mr. Ochiai was plucking one painting from the stack of seven and standing up from his desk. The person who now stood at the door was Hiroto Kasai, the teacher from grade five, class two. He was young, only in his fifth year of teaching.

"Oh hello, Mr. Ochiai. I had a feeling you'd be in your classroom. Ms. Yukawa has been looking for you to discuss morning assembly duty for next week."

Morning assembly happened every Monday, and the teachers took turns to address the students.

"Has she, now," he replied. "I just finished grading artwork. I'll stop by the teachers' lounge before I head over to lead my club's activities."

Mr. Ochiai was in charge of the English debate club, which

was held in a classroom on the same floor as the teachers' lounge. The debate club had less than twenty members, but they all had top grades and no personality or behavioral issues. To Mr. Ochiai, *that* was the kind of role he considered to be his life's work.

In college, he'd majored in Japanese literature, but after making an appearance at his friend's English presentation society, he took an interest in public speaking. Most of his English practice happened through independent study, but his talent for it had been recognized. Now that he'd become an elementary school teacher, he'd received many opportunities to utilize it—such as teaching English in class *and* during club activities.

He glanced at his watch, then gathered the paintings again to make one neat stack, which he placed in the envelope.

"Those paintings are depictions of Kenji Miyazawa's world, right? How did it go?" Mr. Kasai asked, intrigued.

"It took them a while to get used to converting text into imagery. By the time they all turned these in, it took two whole months." He sighed, then mumbled under his breath. "Good grief."

"What if you give them an easier version of the curriculum? Unless you give them something specific to depict like you used to, maybe a character or a motif, it's only going to take up extra time."

Mr. Ochiai scratched his graying hair.

Mr. Kasai's eyes widened with wonder. "But it *is* interesting. It's like getting a peek inside everyone's head."

He smiled. Mr. Ochiai went to leave the classroom.

"Can I see what kinds of paintings your students made? I'd love to reference them for when my class does this exercise," Mr. Kasai said.

"Go ahead."

Mr. Ochiai had already made his selections, so he handed the envelope over. Mr. Kasai opened it on the spot. He leafed through the artwork, occasionally making impressed exclamations such as "Wow!" and "Neat!"

"This one is very unique in approach," he said to himself.

This sparked Mr. Ochiai to glance at the paper in the other teacher's hand. The painting depicted the sky and water on the top and bottom halves of the paper, but the shades of blue were gradually blurred, like a gradient.

It wasn't one of the pieces from the names he'd chosen. This was his first time seeing it.

"Whose is that?" he asked.

Mr. Kasai flipped the painting. "Rin Takai. Oh wow. *She* painted this?"

Rin came from a complicated home life. She was prone to missing school. He'd heard that her grandfather was in a nursing home. The principal had told him not to be too hard on her, so once her grades slipped, he'd given up on her. She wasn't a bad kid, just a quiet one, therefore she never made a strong impression. If he had to choose, he wouldn't say she was bad *or* good. He just didn't think she excelled at anything.

Although the composition of the artwork Mr. Kasai was praising *was* unique, it lacked obedience, and therefore didn't amount to much in his eyes. Given how young the other teacher was, he probably assumed rarity meant excellence. But the longer he kept up his job, the more he'd realize these things were happenstance.

"Ooh, this one is good, too," Mr. Kasai said. Yet again, his eyes roved over a piece that wasn't part of his chosen seven. "The use of color is fantastic. Don't you think?"

As Mr. Ochiai approached, he looked at the name written on the back corner of the artwork. Haruka Mita constantly spent her break time in the library with her nose in a borrowed book. She was practically a ghost in the classroom. Thankfully she didn't seem to have fallen prey to bullying, but she constantly wore a gloomy expression. Frankly, he got the sense that she was hard to interact with.

"But don't you think those are strange color choices for a night sky?" he asked.

The whole surface was coral pink with orange and yellow interspersed.

"Maybe she meant to paint it as Kenji saw it," Mr. Kasai replied, fixated.

"I don't think it's *that* good. It's too individualistic for anyone to have an opinion on it."

"But when you come across a kid who paints like this, it's exciting to imagine what kind of occupation they will grow up to have."

Unfortunately for Rin and Haruka, they weren't the kind of people who could slide into just any occupation. That was only possible for the limited few who demonstrated excellence.

"I'd rather they cultivate more cooperation," he replied.

School was for building relationships that would serve students in their adult lives. A number of students from each class who fit the bill came to mind. *They* were the ones who had bright futures—members of the elementary school student council and class representatives. Their extracurricular positions and the grades they held were easy signs by which to evaluate them.

But Mr. Kasai couldn't tear his eyes away from Haruka's painting. "I envy all of the possible futures that wait ahead of her. But this is why I'm glad I became a teacher. I can help students find their way."

Mr. Ochiai subconsciously let out a snort of laughter at Mr. Kasai's display of naivety.

When Mr. Ochiai entered the teachers' lounge, he found Ms. Yukawa waiting for him.

"You want to discuss the subject of morning assembly,

correct? Sorry to keep you," Mr. Ochiai said. "Mr. Kasai from class two wanted to see the paintings my students submitted."

The best artwork was predetermined based on the student who made it. Mr. Kasai must've had a screw loose to compliment all the strange ones. Surely it was inexperience that contributed to his lack of discernment, and that couldn't be helped. Mr. Ochiai felt sorry for the children subjected to lessons from a teacher like him.

"Oh, I'll bet Mr. Kasai took an interest," Ms. Yukawa said, eyes crinkling behind her glasses to match her warm smile.

"He's young. That reaction is common for anyone so early in a teaching career," Mr. Ochiai replied with disinterest. But her response shocked him.

"That's his area of expertise. Of course he'd want to see some good paintings."

"Huh? What area of expertise?"

"You didn't know? He's been painting since he was a child. He was famous back in his hometown. The principal said he received some sort of major award in his third year of college. In fact, he was recently asked to be a volunteer judge for an art competition. Anyway, he has quite the eye, as you'd expect."

The unexpected information compelled him to mind his tongue, but he managed to squeeze out a response to justify himself.

"So he became a teacher because art was a dead end for him?"

"He told me something a while ago . . ." Apparently, Ms. Yukawa had been curious enough to ask him the same question at one point. "He said that everyone has talent, and it's important for each person to recognize their individual gift and put it to use. He wanted to become an elementary school teacher to help students from all backgrounds and social standings identify hints of their latent skills. He hopes that those hints will make them conscious of actions they can take toward their future in adulthood."

Mr. Ochiai recalled the class reunion he'd attended the month prior. It was the fifteenth anniversary for the students who had graduated from his second year of teaching.

Predictably, the top-performing students had ultimately gone on to become doctors and lawyers and whatnot. A pretty girl who'd sat on the fringes of academic excellence had still managed to become a homemaker *and* a fashion model for a magazine on the side. She'd even shown him a page with her photo.

However, something about the story Ms. Yukawa had mentioned left him unsettled. There *was* one student at the reunion who he couldn't get out of his head.

"Susumu is doing amazingly, Mr. Ochiai. He's the president of a company," one of his former students had told him.

It was Hanabishi—a student he remembered because his father had served on the PTA.

"Oh, enough about me," the man beside him—apparently Susumu—had interjected, smiling shyly. He didn't seem like the president of a company. He gave off the impression of an agreeable young man, to put it nicely.

In that moment, Mr. Ochiai had struggled to place Susumu in his classroom. Even the name—Susumu Hirose—had been lost on him.

"How many hundreds of millions do you bring in every year again? I saw it online," Hanabishi had nudged his friend.

Meanwhile, Mr. Ochiai had pretended to be nonchalant, flipping through their graduation album. One of the attendees had brought it out of nostalgia. It had the photos and names of everyone in their class. He avoided their gazes and desperately searched for the name. The "Susumu Hirose" depicted in the photo resembled the young man who stood in front of him, but even the photo didn't jog his memory. He couldn't recall a child like him, which proved just how much he *hadn't* taken notice of him.

To cast off his irritation, he'd instead made his way to a circular table, where several others had gathered.

"You've grown into impressive people," he'd told the students whose names he remembered.

All to reinforce the fact that he had been right.

Ms. Yukawa's voice brought him back to the present.

"So, have you heard about the reassignments for next year?" she asked.

"We're getting a new teacher fresh out of school, right?" He sighed. "We have our hands full already. It's no small thing for us to be expected to mind an inexperienced teacher, too."

"I heard his academic record is incredible. After he graduated from a Japanese grad school, he went to do research at an American university. Supposedly he's excelled in many areas."

"Academic record alone won't teach him anything. He needs experience."

Mr. Ochiai stuck his nose up, but Ms. Yukawa's response took him aback.

"If we have a teacher who's used to native-level English, the English debate club supervisor will probably change, too. Maybe you'll get to take it easy starting next year, don't you think?"

"Huh? I don't mind continuing to advise the club." He panicked and added, "Besides, the children are making marked improvements with my lessons. I'm sure they'd feel more assured with me at the helm than a new teacher."

Ms. Yukawa tilted her head, looking doubtful. "I'm not so sure. The parents would probably be happier for them to have guidance from a teacher who's spent time in America. You specialize in Japanese literature, anyway."

"I made it this far thanks to diligent independent study. I won't be replaced by an inexperienced teacher with a flashy title and academic record. That's a superficial way to evaluate someone."

The unfair treatment made his blood boil. He took his seat, fuming with rage at how absurd this was.

His gaze fell back onto the paintings he was holding. Something grated in his chest.

Positions and grades were easy signals by which to evaluate them.

Titles, academic record, age . . . all superficial measures of evaluation. This was the same way he'd been treating these children. He shuddered, realizing he was now subject to it.

With no outlet for his anger, he remained dumbfounded, the envelope full of paintings still held tight in his grip. Then he hesitated, unsure whether or not to withdraw them for a second look.

He decided, maybe he should.

7

"Serves him right" seemed like the appropriate phrase to express the satisfaction I felt.

I left my post at the school hallway window and shook out my body. I'd stretched my back to peek inside the teachers' lounge, so now I needed to arch it in a cat pose as much as I could, righting my body back to normal.

Having watched the events unfold successfully, I slipped through the exit and into the outdoors. Once I made it through the center of the schoolyard and beyond the campus grounds, a gust of wind blew by. For a second, I thought I heard commotion in the schoolyard behind me—the sound of Susumu and Hanabishi playing dodgeball.

8

Nijiko cackled as she set the staffing schedule on top of the dresser.

"Just imagining the look on Mr. Ochiai's face when he realized that young teacher was a professional artist is hilarious! *Then* he got dismissed from his adviser role? Talk about a double punch!"

As she pressed my fourth pawprint stamp onto my task chart, I snorted a laugh, too.

"Too bad Susumu and Hanabishi couldn't see it. It was *so* satisfying," I replied.

"True. But I'm sure they're performing splendidly at their jobs. Isn't that enough? Anyway, Fuuta, how did you entrust the soul to two teachers?" I'd acted extra carefully.

While investigating, I'd figured it was impossible to convey the message through just one person. I needed a location—somewhere several people would unknowingly come in contact with the soul. Once I'd come to this decision, I realized that the door to the teachers' lounge was the perfect location.

"Wasn't that risky? Mr. Ochiai could've touched that door, too," Nijiko pointed out.

"That's why I did it when he was in his classroom."

After school, when I saw him grading the artwork in his classroom, I immediately snuck into the teachers' lounge. Thankfully the children had already left campus, so I was able to infiltrate the space without witnesses and successfully transfer the soul to the door.

"Ms. Yukawa, the teacher on morning assembly duty, opened the door first. Then Mr. Kasai touched it next. He's the one who went to find Mr. Ochiai," I explained.

"I see. With the right point of contact, even if Ms. Yukawa touched it first, a bit of the soul would linger behind and transfer to Mr. Kasai, too."

A soul's power never lasted, though. Once Mr. Ochiai arrived at the teachers' lounge, the effect had worn off. When he touched the door, the soul hadn't transferred.

"Yikes! That plan would have me on edge," Nijiko exclaimed. She hugged herself, arms crossed over her chest.

"It all comes down to precision. My whiskers can sense the perfect moment," I boasted, flaring them for her.

I had to admit that *some* chance had been involved in everything working out, but that was fine with me. All's well that ends well, as the saying went.

As I watched Nijiko press her hands to her chest, I recalled what Sky had told me about her.

"Hey. You do this job because you have regrets about a pet cat you once had, don't you?" I asked abruptly.

"I do." She suddenly turned her face downward, seemingly unsurprised that I'd asked. "My cat died because of me."

She explained how her cat had been healthy even in old age—the *really* old age of twenty-two years. She lowered her eyes again as she mentioned how her cat's appetite had vanished a few days before the death.

"That's called a lifespan," I said. "Everyone has one. It wasn't your fault."

"It's not that. I should've stayed home to take care of her. If I had, maybe it wouldn't upset me so much."

"Tell me. What happened?"

Nijiko hung her head for a while before her story began to trickle out.

"I brought her to a pet hospital. She was already so weak, and even though she fought me on it, I forced her into a carrier, anyway."

"Sorry, but I hate the vet, too."

"I'm sure you do. I knew she did, but I didn't know what else to do."

The night Nijiko admitted her cat, she drew her last breath in the hospital.

"If I'd kept her at home, she wouldn't have gone through the trauma. Maybe she would've lived longer. I'm sure she was lonely. I wish I'd been there for her. I wanted to thank her in her last moments before I said goodbye. I've missed her . . ." Tears began to spill from her eyes. "That's why I want to give the cats in the land of blue the little bit of happiness I can. If they have someone in the land of green they want to see, I want to give them that opportunity. That's why I do this job."

Her expression crinkled as she smiled through her tears.

"So that's why," I said.

There was no way her cat thought poorly of her. In fact, she was probably grateful for her. As much as I wanted to say this to Nijiko, though, I couldn't find the right words. I remained unsure of what to say, but then she spoke.

"Have you heard the legend of the rainbow bridge?" she asked, wiping tears away.

She described a legend where departed pets waited at the end of a rainbow bridge to greet their humans once they came to the afterlife.

"That's not a legend. That's basically the truth!" I exclaimed.

The tortoiseshell cat guarded the bridge where the land of green and the land of blue connected—and this café stood there, too. Nijiko giggled at my surprise.

"It's up to the individual whether to believe it. I don't know what the full truth is, either, but I think it's a good thing to jump on the bandwagon of that belief."

"'Pont' means 'bridge' in French, right?"

"Oh my. I'm surprised you know that."

Nijiko was highly impressed with me, but I was only repeating what I'd overheard from a customer. That was my secret. But if the café's name truly meant "bridge," then maybe Nijiko's name—which meant "rainbow child"—wasn't her real name, but a nickname.

"But wouldn't your cat be in the land of blue now? Can't you go search for her?" I asked.

"Unlike humans, it's difficult to pinpoint a cat's location. I can't meet her unless she responds to my messenger cat job listing. But that's too much to ask for. There aren't many cats that would take on such an admirable yet tedious job," she said, casting me a wink.

If Nijiko's pain and regret could be transformed into such a grand act of kindness toward others, then Nijiko's strength and love served as an example to aspire to.

Now that's what makes a good teacher.

TASK FIVE

MESSENGER CAT CURLS UP ON SOMEONE'S LAP

1

Inside Café Pont, a string of words pricked my ears to attention.

"I'm a thief for a living."

"What did she just say?" I said, looking up at the café's exterior.

I'd been curled up outside, sunbathing near the door, when a customer had blurted that confession. I promptly strode to a spot beneath the window and leaped up onto the windowsill.

"What did you just say?" Nijiko asked the woman, visibly puzzled.

It seemed I wasn't the only one at a loss for words. No way she wanted to become complicit in a crime.

The customer, a woman who appeared to be in her mid-forties, casually opened her mouth again to speak. "I run a small gallery out of part of my house," she explained, then named the town.

"That's a coastal town," Nijiko remarked.

Even I recognized the name of the town: Ajisai. Michiru's Mama had been invited to go there on a quick vacation one time. She'd excitedly mentioned that Ajisai had a beautiful temple and that she'd gone to see it. She bought a souvenir for me—a collar with a cute bell on it—but I didn't like accessories. They would compel me to swipe at my throat.

"Aww. It looks so good on you, though," Mama had lamented, but removed it immediately.

The woman continued to describe her gallery store, where she exhibited and sold specific items, such as artwork from an acquaintance of hers and pottery work from a local ceramist.

"Half of my customers are locals, but during the weekends, sightseers tend to drop by. I still wouldn't say business has been booming," she said with a laugh. She described how she'd remodeled the two-story home to accommodate a shop on the first floor and her living space on the second. "My son moved out to go to college, so now it's too much space for just my husband and me."

In the wake of her child's independence, in the midst of all her free time, she'd inherited artwork from her acquaintance—the local artist. The woman then spoke the artist's name.

"I don't know that artist," Nijiko said, tilting her head.

"I'm sure you don't. She was young when she passed away,

so she hadn't become famous. But she made incredible paintings. I started the gallery so I could introduce people to her work."

The customer had majored in art history once upon a time. Given her interest in paintings, she'd developed a habit of touring art museums. She'd never imagined it would become her occupation one day.

"There are aspects to the business that I still don't understand," she continued. "I hadn't pictured myself with my own store before. I was just a housewife, so I'm fumbling a little."

Once she'd opened shop, she expanded her inventory to include products from local craftspeople. Now, she handled all genres of artwork on top of those paintings.

Nijiko's gaze fell to the postcard in her hand. "So who is the person you named here?" she asked.

This woman hadn't put her postcard in the letterbox. She'd decided to hand it to Nijiko and share her story directly, apparently.

"She was my best friend," the woman told her.

"Your friend? I'm sorry to be rude, but is she alive?" Nijiko asked.

Nijiko had to ask. A client's named individual could be from the land of green, too.

The customer replied, "Yes, she's alive and well. According to my other friend, at least."

"Do you know where she is?"

"I've visited her many times. I know where she lives."

Nijiko's tone roughened. "Then why not see her yourself?"

The woman kept her eyes downcast for a while before she finally whispered, "Like I said, I'm a thief. I stole something precious from her."

Nijiko narrowed her eyes as if to pry the words from her. "What do you mean?"

"She and I started off in the same class in fifth grade."

They'd walked home in the same direction; perhaps that was why they became fast friends. They ended up spending their break time together, too. Whenever they went their separate ways after school, they made a huge, tragic deal out of it, waving vigorously. This was despite the fact that they'd see each other the next morning, a mere several hours later.

Once they graduated to middle school, they joined the same after-school art club. They served as each other's sketch models, but they mostly drew manga characters. Though they attended separate high schools and universities, they spent their days off shopping or watching movies. They were similar even in size and stature; they traded clothes, walking around in matching outfits. Perhaps it was the influence of this friend that made our customer fall in love with art museums.

"Our friendship stayed the same even into adulthood," the customer explained further. This best friend of hers was hired at a brokerage firm, where she busted her butt to this day. "I married my college boyfriend around the same time as our graduation, then had my son soon after. That completely changed our places in life."

Yet her best friend still squeezed time out of her busy schedule to celebrate her son's birthday, gift her with the trendiest sweets, and make countless visits to her home.

"I went through a lot raising my son, and many things happened between my husband and I, so there were times when I'd go running to her house."

"Wouldn't one normally find solace with their parents at times like that?" Nijiko asked, sounding confused.

"Yes, but I didn't want to deal with any questions from my parents. My best friend wouldn't push me. And I appreciated that." She gave a small nod, the window reflecting her nostalgic expression.

"You were closer to her than you were to your own blood relatives, then," Nijiko noted.

"I was. My husband knew it, too. Whenever I'd storm out of the house, he would contact her first. He'd always say, 'My wife is over there, isn't she?'"

"Oh dear."

It was as if their souls were tethered. That was the exact same feeling I had with Michiru, Mama, and Papa—an irreplaceable sense of security. Just the thought of it enveloped me in feelings so soft and warm I felt it physically, and started to nod off. There was no way the customer could see me drifting off, but her voice changed suddenly, as if my gesture had underscored her pain.

"But then one day, she just stopped all contact with me," she said.

"Did something happen?" Nijiko asked.

I raised my ears, attentive again.

"When I first opened my shop, I floundered with my own issues for a while, and her department had some personnel changes, too, so we went several months with no contact. It was a busy time for both of us. I didn't think much of it."

"I hear brokerage firms have chaotic seasons with shareholder meetings at the end of the fiscal year."

"They do. When I sent her a text and she didn't respond, I figured she was just too busy. I wasn't contacting her for anything significant enough to warrant a response, anyway."

Meanwhile, time suddenly passed by them in the blink of an eye. Before she knew it, she hadn't heard from her best friend in over a year.

"As you'd expect, I got worried," she went on. "I wondered if something bad had happened."

"I imagine her living alone made that even more concerning."

"It did. I ended up asking someone else to check on her." She explained that a mutual friend still lived in their old neighborhood. "That person said she'd called me a thief."

She ducked her head, ashamed.

"A thief of what?" Nijiko asked. "Her relationship with a man?"

I, too, recalled from a TV drama that female friendships easily fell apart for reasons such as that.

"You would think so," the customer replied. "I imagined it was something like that at first. I thought maybe I'd unknowingly become too friendly with someone important to her."

That *was* possible. Even if this customer hadn't pursued anything, a man could've developed a one-sided crush on her.

"But the more I considered it, the more I realized that couldn't be the reason," she explained. Supposedly her friend hadn't experienced any major changes in her daily life, so the customer had lamented over what she might have missed.

"Maybe it was about an object," Nijiko offered. "Maybe you accidentally kept an important book you borrowed, or something like that."

"That's plausible." The woman cracked a smile. "When we were in high school, I'd borrow manga from her, only for it to end up on my bookshelf. But that went both ways. I'm sure she still has my favorite books in *her* room." It was proof of their friendship, she said. "We lent and borrowed things so frequently that we'd lose track of who it belonged to. We were happy like that."

If they'd been *that* close, where could things have gone wrong?

"This might be presumptuous," the customer added hesitatingly, "but I'd also thought maybe she was jealous of me. I had a husband and son, and I was living a carefree life with no occupation. Yet she was living all on her own. That kind of lifestyle is great when you're young, but as the years passed, I wondered if her feelings about it had changed."

"But she must've found purpose in her job, right? If she was that intensely involved in it?"

"Exactly. That's why I don't really think that was the reason, either. She's not the kind of person to want what I had. Thinking back, she was happy for *me* that my son was headed off to college. She knew how much I'd fretted over raising and educating him. She reassured me that once he had a job lined up, I could finally let go and dedicate some time to myself."

"Could there be a distance component to losing contact? If you think about it, traveling so far to see you *would* get tiresome."

"No. She liked that I'd moved. Maybe she was also tired of city life, because she was so happy to come visit me. She said the view was gorgeous. This discrepancy is what prompted me to start looking into when *exactly* she cut contact."

"I see," Nijiko said attentively.

The customer's voice lowered. "She stopped talking to me after I started the gallery. That was two years ago."

"Has your friend ever visited the gallery?"

"Once, during the grand opening. I had my hands full with management, so maybe I hadn't noticed her demeanor change. But once I *really* thought back on that day, I realized that that was when it had started," the customer mumbled, hanging her head with a lonely expression. "And then a memory struck me. Back in middle school, she'd said something to me in the art room."

"What did she say?"

I leaned forward to listen, too. My ears, tail, *and* whiskers stood pin straight.

"All of the club members' drawings had been displayed for critique. As we'd looked at each one, she'd mentioned that she wanted to open a small art gallery someday, in a town where you could clearly see the ocean. She said it was her dream."

The customer's voice then took on the bright tone of a middle-school girl, as if she was visualizing her dreams for the future.

"I see. You're now living your friend's dream," Nijiko replied softly, as if to share in the heart-to-heart.

"That's why I want to see her and apologize."

Nijiko inclined her head for a moment. "Should you, though? Is there any *need* for you to apologize?" she asked. "It's not as if there can be only one seaside gallery in the world. Many of them already exist. If your friend wants to open one, she should just do it. You put in the work for *your* gallery. You built connections over time and made it a reality.

Those were the fruits of *your* labor. I don't think there's any need for you to apologize."

"But it's the reason she's angry."

"Could the problem be that you pretended not to remember that it had been her dream? You can't deny that on some level you actually *did* remember, so you decided to usurp her dream first. Am I right?"

"Usurp her dream? I'd never . . ." She waved her hand in front of her face as if to vehemently deny the accusation.

"Really?" Nijiko pressed. Her tone was calm, but she must've struck a nerve in the customer on a deep level, because she slowly raised her head.

"Maybe *I* was the jealous one," she admitted. "Many subordinates and superiors at her company love her. She's walking her own life path to the fullest. She has plenty of money to use as freely as she wants. She always looks great and buys the trendiest things. Compared to that, I'm a boring housewife. All I ever did was fret over the price of cucumbers, raise a child, and wear the same clothes for years. So when I opened my gallery, I finally felt like I could accomplish something, too."

"You *both* can." Nijiko looked at her with fondness in her eyes. "Why don't you meet up with her and reminisce about old times? Maybe bring up how the gallery was a mutual dream, and talk about who you both are now."

"I wonder if she'd be willing to see me," the customer replied anxiously.

"There are many people with whom we want to reminisce, but aren't able to. You two aren't among them. Go see her in person, okay?"

With a firm but encouraging nod, Nijiko offered the survey card back to the customer.

2

Once the customer had left, I entered Café Pont. Messenger cats weren't allowed inside during business hours, but Nijiko didn't get mad at us if we poked our heads in when no customers were around.

"Sheesh. She startled me by calling herself a thief. You should make her repent to us for that," I remarked.

Nijiko noted the lack of foot traffic. "Looks like the birds have flown the coop for good today. I'd be crazy as a cuckoo if I didn't close up early," she said.

I'd never seen a cuckoo bird before, but I'd heard they were also called *Cuculus canorus*.

"You received lots of request cards, though," I said, impressed.

"About half of these targets can be approached if the customer makes an effort on their own. They just don't *believe* they can meet with them."

"That old story, huh? But do you think that last customer will be okay?"

Her best friend clearly didn't want to see her. So would a future meeting ever happen?

"She'll manage," Nijiko replied. "Talking through the good memories they have together is bound to be beneficial. Unlike situations like this one." She flipped over a survey card for me to take a look. I read the card aloud. "'I want to see my mother, who has dementia, and reminisce with her.'"

"*This* is what it truly means to be unable to 'meet' someone. It's when you're at your wit's end," Nijiko explained.

In this case, when the target couldn't even *recognize* the client. And that from a beloved mother, too. Just the thought of it pained my heart. If Michiru had ever failed to recognize me, I wouldn't have been able to take it.

"Do you understand?" Nijiko asked, nudging me out of my silence.

I nodded.

"Then I'll task you with this one. It's in your paws now," she ordered with a smirk.

How was I supposed to arrange a meeting with a human with fuzzy memories? This would be a tricky one. But I wanted to try. I knew that if my imagination—and my and Nijiko's actions—could bring someone just a bit of relief, it would still be worth it.

"Your imagination has gotten much stronger, you know," Nijiko said, watching me with a motherly gaze.

I jumped off the dresser and padded over to the fireplace, where I'd take a nap before my mission. I would work out a plan later.

3

The client, Kozue Hosaka, was a woman in her sixties who wanted to meet her mother, Satsuki Komai. Kozue's survey card included the name of the nursing home where Satsuki, ninety years old, resided.

"If I go here, I can meet the client *and* her target," I told myself.

Or so I assumed. Things didn't always pan out that easily.

As soon as I arrived at the home, I was able to pinpoint the location of her mother's room, but I snuck over to the "pet room" first. The interior resembled a cat café.

I had this task in the bag.

This home kept cats and dogs called "therapy pets." Animals like this were often utilized at hospitals to bring psychological relief to the patients, but according to the pets I approached, they were part of a program to alleviate anxiety symptoms for dementia. Many of the animals here belonged to the land of green, but several of them had temporarily transferred in from the land of blue. As part of my investigation, I diligently listened to their stories of Satsuki.

"Satsuki? She's a kind and gentle person," said a tabby cat who looked just like me. Apparently, she often let him curl up on her lap.

After I told him the details of my task, a nearby cat *and* dog chimed in.

"Her family comes to visit her every day, so you should be able to see them," the cat said.

"But that's her *son* and his wife," the dog retorted. "And only the wife comes on weekdays. They come together on weekends. We've never met Satsuki's daughter."

"She has moments where she remembers things, and times when she doesn't," said a third pet, who seemed befuddled by that detail.

I decided to store this information in my head for the time being, then headed for Satsuki's room.

4

After a bit of loitering outside her room, the door opened. It was mealtime, so she must've been about to go to the cafeteria. Here I was thinking she wouldn't be able to function on her own; Satsuki's inconsistent memories had been a hot topic in the pet room, but it seemed she could at least move around the facility unattended.

"Oh, Kuu. You came all the way to my room for me," Satsuki said.

"Who's Kuu? I'm Fuuta," I thoughtlessly blurted. Just as I did, I realized that maybe her getting my name wrong was a stroke of good luck. With my identity mistaken, I could observe Satsuki up close.

"Come inside my room," she offered.

I had no idea whether the therapy cats were allowed to leave the pet room at will, but I couldn't care less. Satsuki thought I was Kuu, the tabby cat I'd just met. I promptly trotted inside with her.

Satsuki allowed me to sit on her lap and petted me. It seemed she'd completely forgotten about going to the cafeteria. I felt sorry for interrupting her plan, but the facility's caregivers were bound to deliver her meal, or at least come calling for her. Until then, I'd play the role of Kuu.

"Would you like a treat, Kuu?" Satsuki asked. She withdrew a pack of dried sardines from her drawer.

I instantly swished my tail and purred. But why did she have dried sardines? How strange.

"Satoru brought me these dried sardines," she explained. "He said calcium is good for the bones and teeth, so I should eat them whenever I need a snack. Have you ever met Satoru?"

Contrary to Satoru's intentions behind the sardines, Satsuki had no teeth left in her mouth. She had dentures, but she must've only worn them right before a meal.

"I can't eat anything this tough anymore," she lamented. "But my son is so sweet. My one and only child . . ."

Tears welled in her eyes. I couldn't tell if they were because she was happy or sad. Humans tended to cry on both occasions. I'd heard that they cried easier as they got older, too. Was this what this was? Cats didn't exactly get "sad," at least not in the same way, so I didn't understand much about crying.

I realized that Satsuki had just mentioned her son—Satoru—but not her daughter, Kozue. She'd said he was her only child.

So, she really had forgotten she had a daughter.

Furnished with only a bed and table, the tiny room felt bleak. However, there was a small butsudan in the back. That Buddhist altar was likely where the smell of incense originated from. The picture frame in the front of the butsudan displayed a man with a humble expression. It must've been Satsuki's husband, as well as Satoru and Kozue's father. I didn't see any other family pictures in the room.

I stayed curled up snug on Satsuki's lap. It'd been a while since I'd basked in the happiness of human attention. Finally starting to relax, I decided to close my eyes for a catnap, until I heard someone suddenly knocking on the door. A woman entered.

"Mom? Are you here?" she asked.

Was it Kozue? I hoped so, but my hopes were dashed quickly.

"Oh hello, Hanae. Is it just you today?" Satsuki answered.

"Satoru is at work during the weekdays," her daughter-in-law replied.

I could tell this was a common exchange for them. Hanae sounded used to the question.

"One of the caregivers said to hurry over for your meal," Hanae said gently, now noticing me on Satsuki's lap. "Oh gosh. Is that one of the pet room cats? You'll get in trouble if you bring them here on your own," she chastised.

I felt Satsuki flinch from where I sat on her lap. "But Kuu was in front of my door . . ."

Satsuki was flustered and confused. I couldn't cause any further trouble for her. I acted innocent and slipped out of the door Hanae had left open, hearing tut-tutting in my wake.

What was I supposed to do for this task?

Still without a starting point, I dragged my paws back to Café Pont. I hoped to find a fellow messenger cat, but none of them were lounging in front of the café. Even worse, a TEMPORARILY CLOSED sign had been posted on the door. I tried to peek inside, but the shop was quieter than a mouse. With Nijiko gone, even the fireplace was cold.

The warmth of Satsuki's lap lingered on my body. It brought me back to the times when Michiru would pet me. My head drooped with a sudden surge of loneliness.

"If I were a human, would this be a moment I would cry alone?" I wondered.

I went to search for Natsuki in the hopes of confiding in her, but was unsuccessful. Maybe that was a good thing; she'd only see me at my most pathetic.

"I think she mentioned she'd taken a part-time job in the land of green," I mumbled.

I pulled myself together and tried to recall the last time I'd spoken to her. I *had* happened to run into her recently. She'd mentioned the witch cats were busy lately, especially with Halloween coming up.

"I still can't fly freely on a broomstick," she'd explained. "I'm just going to sit on a broomstick as a café decoration."

Somewhere in the land of green, she would be dangling in a random café's window display.

"Does that mean you'll be there until Halloween is over?" I'd asked, slightly worried.

"The café will only be open starting the night of the crescent moon until the night of the full moon. That means the gig should only last about two weeks in October."

"Oh. That's all?"

The anticlimactic answer had made me sigh with relief.

"What kind of café operates for such a short time, anyway?"

Nijiko didn't run Café Pont within standard hours, either, but she did more business than *that*.

"It's supposed to be an aesthetic but easygoing café. I'm excited to work there," Natsuki had replied, brimming with energy. "I heard the café owner takes care of a black tomcat named Mackerel. Isn't it funny that a cat is named after a fish?"

For some reason her enjoyment had made it harder to smother my jealousy.

That conversation had taken place about ten days ago, so she'd probably be back soon. Natsuki was clearly making steady growth as a witch cat. It seemed like I was the only one not progressing. As confident as I was, I felt a little hopeless.

I used my claw to pick at a piece of sardine that had gotten stuck at the back of my teeth. I licked it—and the circumference of my mouth. The pleasant fragrance of sardines and incense overlapped.

The mattresses in the nursing home were pretty stiff. Still, it was nice and warm under Satsuki's arm as she dozed.

Nearby voices pulled me from the edge of sleep, but I couldn't focus on them in my cozy position. I poked my head out from under the covers to find Hanae standing next to the bed.

"Oh dear. It's the pet room cat again," said Hanae, turning away from the man at her side. She looked startled to see me as I jumped down to the floor with a soft thump, where I licked my fur to fix my coat. The man who stood next to her must've been Satoru.

"Are the pets allowed to roam the rooms at will?" he asked.

"I wonder. He was here last time, too. I thought your mother brought him in. I warned her not to, but now that I think about it, she wouldn't have done that. He's a therapy pet, so it makes sense for them to enter the rooms like this as a form of rehab, doesn't it?"

Satoru had asked the question, but as Hanae explained her theory, he appeared to have already lost interest.

"I came all this way. Will she be asleep the whole time?" His sigh suggested he was more irritated than disappointed. That same attitude was reflected in his eyes. It made me feel a bit upset for Satsuki.

"When she's calm, her behavior is completely normal. She's very aware of people like you and me. But one of the caregivers thinks it's cyclical. It feels like her condition changes once every two weeks or so."

The breeze that drifted through the window delivered a chill that made my body shiver.

"By the way, my sister sent me this text," Satoru said, withdrawing his smartphone from his jacket pocket.

"Your sister? What did she say?"

He tried to show Hanae the phone screen, but she got up to close the window instead. He lowered his gaze to the phone and began to read the text aloud.

"'How is Mom doing? I'm sorry to leave all of her care to both of you. I watch the facility from afar every day.'"

Silence fell over the room. Hanae was the one to break it.

"Maybe she wants to see her. Why don't we let her, just once?" she suggested.

I flexed my whiskers in approval, but Satoru shook his head.

"We'd better not. Their relationship was bad to begin with. Letting them meet will only cause chaos. Her memories of having a daughter are murky now, but because of that, she's stable."

"Your sister hasn't seen your mother since her divorce, right?"

"No, they cut contact even before that. Mom was so against the marriage, but Kozue did it anyway, remember? Mom got so angry that once Kozue was married, she told her that she didn't have a daughter anymore. That sham of an elopement only lasted for a year before they got divorced, so you can't really blame Mom for giving up on her, either. Kozue didn't seem to want her maiden name back, anyway."

"Is she alone now?"

"I think so."

"What do you think she meant by 'always watching from afar'?"

"What do you mean?"

"That's what she wrote in that text. She watches the facility every day. Maybe she lives in the neighborhood."

"I don't think she does. Maybe she passes through now and then?"

A knock on the door interrupted them, a caregiver sticking her head through the entrance. The conversation ended there.

"I see Satsuki's son came today. Thanks for checking in on her," said the caregiver. Her tone was brisk.

I took this moment to slip through the gap of the open door and into the hallway. Satoru's voice followed me from a distance.

"She's been asleep all day . . ."

5

I left the nursing-home grounds to roam the surrounding area. What had Kozue meant when she wrote she watched from afar every day? *Improve your imagination.* I pondered potential answers.

Did Kozue go on a walk here every day, like Satoru suggested? I didn't think that was likely. She must've been watching from a nearby apartment window that he didn't know about.

Could I see it?

I stopped and looked around, my gaze pausing at a storefront across the street. The building was home to a drycleaning service. I bounded to the opposite sidewalk, avoiding traffic along the way, then stopped in front of the store. A customer and an employee spoke at the counter on the other side of the automatic door.

"You're leaving one beige sweater with us, then?" asked the employee.

"Yes. I was trying to swap out my seasonal clothes, but I freaked out when I found this sweater I'd left dirty from last year stuffed in the back of the closet!"

The customer's laughter echoed.

"Well, the temperature sure dropped suddenly. No one knows for sure what to wear at the turn of the season," the employee replied, matching the customer's jovial demeanor. The customer must've been a regular.

"It set in early for sure. We're about to enter the festival season. Have you received any lottery tickets from local businesses in the mail yet?" the customer asked.

"I don't live in the area. My commute is over an hour away by train," the employee replied.

"You come from *that* far?"

"I have a connection here—my mother—she's a patient at the nursing home across the street."

"I see. It must be a relief that you can help take care of her, too."

The employee was about to respond when someone shouted from the back of the store, cutting her off.

"Kozue!"

So that *was* her. Kozue Hosaka. She'd been working at this store to watch the nursing home every single day.

"I've got this," I told myself. My fur stood on end as I amped myself up. But it wasn't just my body that appeared double its usual size. My tail had puffed up all the way to the tip, as well.

6

First, I had to figure out how to retrieve Satsuki's soul.

If her memories were fuzzy, that probably meant part of her soul resided in the land of blue. However, she wasn't a resident quite yet, and incomplete souls weren't just floating around, waiting for me to grab them out of thin air.

Hanae *did* mention her condition fluctuated regularly, though. Could there be a pattern to it?

I kept walking as I mulled it over—until my paws met something crunchy. There were leaves, fallen and scattered from the ginkgo tree that stood in the center of a public park. The season really *was* changing. I recalled how Kozue had phrased it.

The turn of the season . . .

I halted amid the yellow leaves.

Humans in the land of blue could approach the land of green during Higan, a seven-day period that occurred in the spring and again in the fall. The day at the center of each period marked the Spring Equinox and Autumnal Equinox, respectively. During the Autumn and Spring Equinoxes, daytime and nighttime became the same length, thanks to the movement of the sun, and that was when the heavens and earth were closest; people in the land of green would use this time to do special things like visit graves.

I knew the customs well. At Michiru's house, I'd eaten ohagi—a rice ball covered with anko—during Higan. I didn't know about other cats, but surprisingly, I'd *loved* the sweetly stewed azuki beans used to make anko. Michiru would let me lick bits of ohagi from her fingertips. It was *very* tasty.

In the springtime, a different term was used for that exact same food: botamochi. Mama once told Michiru that the different names came from flowers that bloomed during each respective season. I had a distinct memory of her telling Michiru that the Spring and Autumnal Equinoxes were each one of the twenty-four solar terms that occurred over a year. I'd thought that meant we'd get to eat ohagi twenty-four times a year, but I was sorely disappointed to learn that that wasn't the case.

The twenty-four solar terms simply divided the year into twenty-four "seasons." Which meant each new "season" lasted for about fifteen days.

Hanae had told Satoru that she suspected Satsuki's condition changed once every two weeks. If so . . .

It wouldn't be so out of the question for human souls to gain the ability to traverse the two worlds based on the changing solar terms. Granted, I had no real evidence to back up my theory. Still convinced of my hunch, I headed back to the nursing home.

A calendar had been left on the reception desk. It incorporated the Rokuyō—the six-day lunar calendar, which marked days with ranging degrees of luck, like taian and tomobiki—as well as the twenty-four solar terms. The next season would start the day after tomorrow.

"I'd better hurry."

I dashed past the lobby—only to smack into the automatic door before it had a chance to open. I staggered backward and realigned myself at the center. Then, the door opened for me.

While I sat curled up on Satsuki's lap, Hanae entered the room at her usual arrival time.

"He's completely attached to you now," Hanae remarked, casting me a tired look.

"You're a good boy, Kuu," Satsuki said to me.

She spoke as if she hadn't heard Hanae, and instead continued to stroke my back. It was a struggle to keep awake. Here I was, on the clock, about to sink into the land of dreams.

I had to force my eyelids apart or they'd close on their own. I kept watch over the room with half-open eyes.

The paper cup on the small bedside table held iced coffee, which Hanae had just purchased from the vending machine. Hanae had taken a sip, then faced the television stand as she started sorting through laundry.

Now was my chance.

I flicked my whiskers pin-straight, adjusted my body precisely, then leaped up on the side table. I extended my left paw and swiped the cup. It tipped over with a hollow *plock*, the coffee spilling all over the hem of Satsuki's light pink gown.

Hanae turned around, panicked. "Oh no! Mom, are you okay?"

Before she could get angry at me, I slipped out of reach. Her yelling must've echoed through the hallway, because a caregiver came running. I dodged her feet and left the room just as she poked her head inside.

"What's the matter?" she asked.

After such a thrilling event, my heart was racing—a rare occurrence for me. I let my breathing settle, then quietly returned to the door, focusing my ears on the conversation inside.

"It splashed near her feet, so nothing landed on her," Hanae explained to the caregiver, "but her gown is dirty, and it can't be washed with water."

She sounded troubled, which made me feel bad for her, but she'd have to forgive me this once.

"Why don't we send it out for dry cleaning? Though our next batch only goes out on Monday," the caregiver replied apologetically.

"Monday? But it wouldn't come back until three days after that, right? She loves this gown. I have an identical spare that she can change into, but that's in the wash, too," Hanae said frantically.

The caregiver spoke softly as if to ease her mind. "If you need it rushed, why don't you take it to the dry cleaner's across the street? I'm pretty sure they have next-day service."

I tailed Hanae as she unknowingly rushed to Kozue's, the gown in tow. The smell of coffee on the hem reached all the way to my nose.

Just as Hanae vanished behind the automatic door, I heard Kozue's voice.

"Welcome," she said.

"Kozue!" Hanae exclaimed, sounding startled to see her sister-in-law. "So, you've been working here, then." She nodded as if in understanding.

Kozue's voice dropped. "I'm sorry I can't help out with my mother."

"This gown is your mother's. Can I get it rushed?"

"This is . . . Wow. She's actually using it."

"Huh? You know about this gown?"

"I gave it to her for her birthday, back when I still lived with her. It was sold as a pair in a bargain pack, but Mom called it wasteful and never wore them."

"They're her favorites. If she doesn't wear them, she gets unsettled. I had no idea they came from you," Hanae said softly.

"We should be able to have it cleaned by tomorrow." Kozue's voice took on a businesslike tone, suddenly brightening, but with no heart. "What time will you be here? I'll make sure it's ready for you."

7

The next day, I waited in front of the cleaner's for Hanae to arrive. Yesterday had been the solar term known as Soukou, or First Frost. I'd already safely retrieved Satsuki's soul from the land of blue. My plan was to transfer it to Hanae so that she could convey Satsuki's message in her conversation with Kozue.

Though the road to get here had been hectic, my nose stuffed up and I sniffled, full of satisfaction that I could finally convey Satsuki's message.

But Hanae was late.

Her pickup time at the cleaner's came and went, but Hanae didn't emerge from across the street. I worried that she might've arrived while my gaze had drifted elsewhere, but that couldn't have happened. I'd held my chest puffed up and my eyes wide open today.

The phone inside the shop rang.

"Hello, you've reached White Cleaners," Kozue said into the phone. "Yes, I understand. We'd discussed a pickup time of ten A.M., but she hasn't arrived yet."

She was talking about Hanae. Relief loosened the knot in my chest. She hadn't slipped past me, after all. Granted I really, *really* had been keeping careful watch. No catnaps to be seen here. None at all.

"What?" Kozue's voice took on a bewildered tone. "Delivery? We can, but . . ."

I worked my imagination to the brink.

This is what had likely occurred: Due to unforeseen circumstances, Hanae had become unable to pick up the cleaned garment. And so she'd asked someone else to call ahead and request the garment for delivery.

"Yes, I'm Kozue Hosaka, but . . . Yes. I'm the one who helped her yesterday."

After that, she only offered short responses like, "Yes," and "Understood," then hung up the phone. Kozue exhaled a sigh so deep and troubled that it reached even my ears outside the store.

She appeared to be working alone today.

Kozue hung a sign on the door that read, WE'LL BE RIGHT BACK. PLEASE WAIT MOMENTARILY, then left the store. She carried the gown in a plastic bag bearing the dry cleaner's name on it.

I reacted nimbly, immediately following her. I felt like the cat detective from a mystery novel I'd once found on Michiru's bookshelf. That had been a blue-eyed Siamese cat, though.

As for Kozue, she didn't have far to go. The building was just across the street, yet she stopped several times along the way to take deep, shuddering breaths and put her hands on her temples. Even when she stepped foot onto the nursing-home grounds, she struggled to make it to the front door. She couldn't have been lost, but she paced unnaturally, as if to backtrack on the path she'd taken to get here.

I wanted to tell her, "The reception desk is straight ahead!" but even I could tell her hesitation wasn't about where things were located. This was about her mother.

After several rounds of indecisive pacing, she finally strode up to the entrance. She spoke at the reception window.

"I'm from White Cleaners. I brought the dry cleaning that Mrs. Komai requested." Her voice came out hurried.

"Oh yes. You're from the cleaner's," the caregiver replied. "I'm sorry, but could I ask you to bring it directly to the room? It's right up those stairs—"

"You want *me* to bring it?" Kozue interrupted, shocked.

"Yes. Mrs. Komai—the daughter-in-law—asked for that.

It seems to be a private garment, so I suspect they don't want us to see it. Sorry to bother you with it, but she said she'd feel better if the woman who accepted the garment delivered it directly," the caregiver said simply. Seemingly busy, she promptly returned to work.

Kozue stood still for a moment, puzzled, but she couldn't stay there forever. She'd left the cleaner's halfway through the day, after all. She lifted her shoulders, inhaled deeply through her nose, then exhaled slowly. After a few moments, she proceeded carefully up the stairs, where she finally stood in front of Satsuki's door and knocked.

"I brought your dry cleaning," she announced, then pulled open the sliding door.

I slipped through the gap to find Satsuki sitting on her chair, gazing out the window. I jumped onto her lap.

"Hello, Kuu. Welcome," Satsuki said to me.

I gazed up at her friendly face and let out a spoiled meow. I flicked my tail, sliding the entire length against her. The piece of her soul that I'd brought from the land of blue entered her—and made her whole.

Satsuki blinked and looked up sharply.

"One of your family members requested this dry cleaning. I'll place it over here," Kozue said, having entered the room. She kept her eyes downcast as she set the bag on the table. Her hair curtained her face making it difficult for me to see her expression from where I was. Which meant Satsuki couldn't see it, either.

"Thank you," Satsuki replied gently.

Kozue turned her back on her mother and went to leave the room—but then Satsuki spoke again.

"Could you help me put that gown on?" She smiled like a little girl. "Wearing it makes me feel good. I don't relax without it."

Kozue seemed to hesitate, but eventually found her words. "Your son's wife told me that it's your favorite. That's why she asked us to clean it in a rush."

A calm expression surfaced on Kozue's face as she spoke. She slowly withdrew the nightgown from the bag and brought it behind Satsuki's chair, where she quietly helped her into it.

Only I, from my position on Satsuki's lap, could see the tears that sprung into Kozue's eyes. Satsuki was facing forward, unaware of her daughter's expression behind her.

"Thank you," Satsuki said, lightly ducking her head in a bow. Kozue didn't respond, so Satsuki spoke again. "Thank you. Thank you for coming."

Once Kozue left the room, I remained on Satsuki's lap while she stroked my back, confiding in me.

"I've been keeping a secret. I have an adorable daughter."

She kept going. "No parent wouldn't cherish their daughter, and yet I . . . but she seems okay now. I'm relieved."

I hoped someday I could convey these words to Kozue, but that was for another time. I needed to commit a bit more devotion to my craft first.

I continued to rest on Satsuki's lap; it was *so* comfortable that I fell asleep. So much so that once I woke up, the sky had gone dark. I needed to return to Café Pont to give my report or Nijiko would worry.

As I made my way to the door, Satsuki came over and slid it open for me. But not before she gave me a dried sardine as a treat.

"You brought her to me, didn't you?" she said. "Thank you, Kuu's look-alike."

She cast me a playful wink.

I had no idea when she'd found me out, or whether she'd known the truth from the start, but it didn't matter either way.

I wanted to say goodbye to the pet room before I left, but my scent was bound to tip them off to the fact that I'd gotten a treat. I made my way straight for the front door instead, and gave my doppelgänger Kuu a silent word of thanks from my heart.

8

"You completed a difficult task all by yourself," Nijiko praised me.

Finally, my task chart boasted five pawprint stamps.

"Get going," she said. "It's your turn now."

EPILOGUE

Delivery people would always be allies to us cats.

It'd only been five months since I'd last left Michiru's house, but seeing the persimmon tree in the garden made the memories rush back with such fervency, I almost couldn't stand it.

The health of the persimmon tree tended to fluctuate with the years of abundant and poor harvest—also known as a "heavy harvest" and "light harvest." Michiru's Papa had been so disappointed when the tree had failed to produce much fruit last autumn, but this year, the branches drooped magnificently with the weight of persimmons.

As I gazed up at them fondly, I heard a truck approaching the curb in front of the house.

"That's the delivery service," I said excitedly, scurrying over.

The driver descended from the truck, and without missing a beat, I rubbed my body along his legs. The tip of my tail touched the sneakers he wore, and in an instant, I'd transferred my own soul into the deliveryman.

It was a strange thing, entrusting one's own soul to someone else.

In a messenger cat's line of work, it was almost unheard of. But today was special.

I was the client, and *I* was the one tasked to fulfill it.

Now embodied by the deliveryman, I glanced down at my uniform. *Huh?* I glanced back at the truck parked on the side of the street. Neither the uniform nor truck had the familiar cat logo on it. Instead, the name of another shop was written in horizontal letters. I'd expected a standard mail delivery service to come help me, but it seemed this man worked for a specific business.

"Nijiko had told me this window would be fine, though," I said to myself, confused.

When I'd told Nijiko about my plan back in Café Pont, she'd done some digging to find me a proper messenger to inhabit at the right moment. She had me convinced that the messenger would be a mail service worker, but maybe I'd heard her incorrectly.

Either way, I'd already transferred my soul. Embracing

my new deliveryman form, I strode triumphantly toward the front door of Michiru's house, and pressed the intercom button built into the entrance.

"Hello! I have a delivery for you."

"Coming!" someone called out immediately. It was Mama's gentle voice. I suppressed my urge to jump for joy.

Papa's voice sounded inside the house, too. "Is that the bakery?"

Wait. Bakery?

I dropped my gaze to look at the box in my hands. Now that I was looking at it again, I realized I'd seen this logo before. *That's right.* This was the bakery I'd visited during one of my tasks as a messenger cat. The one that was famous for cream puff cakes.

Inside the house, I heard Papa continue to talk. "I passed a bakery during work today. There was a massive line, so I didn't think I'd have time to stop and buy anything. But I dropped by on my way home just in case. They told me they'd just finished baking an extra cream puff cake, and that they'd deliver it once it was ready."

"Really?" Michiru replied.

Even now, her excitement tempted me to barge inside the house and nudge her until she petted my head.

"What's the bakery called?" Mama asked.

"Uh, Amboise, I think," Papa replied.

"That's a famous one. They're popular for cream puffs."

Mama sounded perplexed. "But I've never heard of them delivering fresh-baked extras to people."

Only now did I notice that an order ticket had been taped to the cake box, with a small message typed in the "notes" field. SET ASIDE FOR NIJIKO. Heck, it'd even been stamped with her special cat seal.

Thank you, Nijiko.

I swore to arrange a meeting between her and her pet cat one of these days. Someday, I would grant *her* wish.

With my vow in mind, I solidified my grip on the cake box and waited for the front door to open.

Before I knew it, Michiru was standing in front of me.

"I'll take that," she said brightly.

Her hair had grown longer since I'd last seen her. She looked a little more grown up, too—was it makeup? She also wasn't wearing her glasses, which changed her entire look. She must've switched to contact lenses. She looked charming. And best of all, happy and healthy. There was so much I wanted to say to her, but right now, only one thing I *needed* to say.

"Happy birthday!"

I said it with every bit of heart I could muster, and handed her the box. The relief from *finally* saying it hit me so hard, I got drowsy. Panicked, I pressed my lips tight against each other to collect myself. "Please stamp or sign for it *meow*."

Biting back that yawn must've turned *now* into *meow*.

"Okay. Wait a minute, please," she replied.

As Michiru headed for the dining room, I saw her quickly lift the lid. I couldn't help but smile. Michiru might've looked a little older, but she was still a spoiled kid with an unshakable sweet tooth at heart.

"Wow, this looks delicious! There are four pieces, too," she exclaimed then turned her delighted expression toward me.

"Why are there four? I only ordered three," Papa said, sounding confused. He rose from his seat to go check the order receipt, but Michiru interrupted him.

"I get it," she whispered.

She returned to me at the entrance, where I still stood in the deliveryman's body. Instead of her stamp, she handed me a paper plate. On the plate sat the top of a cream puff, heaped high with cream filling.

"Here you go. Happy birthday," Michiru said warmly.

She smiled at me with her teeth, just like she had as a child.

Meanwhile, back at Café Pont, Sky had dropped in to see Nijiko. The two of them were deep in conversation—which, of course, Fuuta had no idea was occurring.

"Do you think he's meeting his human right about now?" Nijiko pondered.

"He said today is her twentieth birthday," Sky replied.

"Fuuta said they'd always celebrated his birthday on the same day. He'd promised they would spend her twentieth birthday together. He wanted to keep that promise."

Sky sounded impressed. *"Now* it makes sense why he worked so hard as a messenger cat."

"Hey. Take a look at this."

Nijiko handed Sky one of the *Who do you wish to meet?* survey cards.

Sky's eyes widened upon seeing what was written on the paper. "Oh wow. She came here?"

"It seems so. I don't remember which customer left the card, though. Just keep it a secret from Fuuta," she said, bringing a finger to her upturned lips.

"It *does* seem better left a secret," he replied, matching her smile.

He pushed back to her the piece of paper, which read:

Client's name (front): *Michiru.*

Desired target (back): *Fuuta.*

Once I returned to cat form, I hid myself in the garden under the shade of the persimmon tree, lapping up the cream that Michiru had shared with me.

After a lick or ten, I heard a voice calling for me. I turned my head, glancing around, but didn't see anyone nearby. Even the cake deliveryman, free of my soul, must've returned to the bakery by now. He and the truck had disappeared. Just my imagination, then.

But as I scooped up the remaining cream with my paws, I heard the voice again.

"Fuuta! Over here!"

It came from *above*. I looked up, beyond the heavy persimmons, and spotted a black object flying past. If I squinted, I could *just* make out the shape of a black cat riding a broomstick. *Natsuki*. She was mounting a single-rider broom all by herself. She waved her paw, happy as could be.

I see. She'd gained her independence.

"I'll give you a ride on the back sometime!" she exclaimed.

What a cheeky cat. Clearly her confidence had grown beyond the level she'd aspired to.

The view of the garden probably looked different from Natsuki's broomstick. All the crying and worrying must've looked insignificant against such a vast, expansive world. The view from the sky didn't sound half bad at all.

But I stayed down here for a few moments longer, savoring the taste of the cream around my mouth.

I'd completed my fifth task and received my reward. The seven-month waiting period had passed, as well, which allowed me to traverse both worlds at my leisure. Still, I decided to continue my job at Café Pont for a little while longer.

It wasn't because I'd taken a personal interest in people's happiness, exactly. It wasn't even because I enjoyed the gratitude I received for helping others come together. It was simply because the treats Nijiko gave me, and having a warm fireplace near which to sleep, gave me bliss.

That was all there was to it.